AN UNSEEN SHOOTIST

Longarm was already prone, with his elbows spread and his Winchester cocked and aimed in the right general direction. So he held on to his edge by not even breathing hard enough to stir the stems above him.

A million years crept by. Then a distant voice called out to him, "We see you there, stranger! Stand up with your hands polite and tell us what you're doing in these parts!"

Longarm did no such thing. Assholes who fired on anyone using a public right-of-way in broad day could hardly be trusted not to gun another asshole who gave them such a swell chance . . .

TABOR EVANS

LONGARM

AND THE SHOSHONI SILVER

JOVE BOOKS, NEW YORK

LONGARM AND THE SHOSHONI SILVER

A Jove Book / published by arrangement with
the author

PRINTING HISTORY
Jove edition / December 1992

ISBN: 0-515-10997-5

Jove Books are published by The Berkley Publishing Group,
200 Madison Avenue, New York, New York 10016.
The name "JOVE" and the "J" logo
are trademarks belonging to Jove Publications, Inc.

PRINTED IN THE UNITED STATES OF AMERICA

10 9 8 7 6 5 4 3 2 1

LONGARM

AND THE
SHOSHONI SILVER

Chapter 1

The question was whether Blue Tooth Tanner spoke true or false when he said he wasn't hungry after fifteen hours aboard the westbound Burlington overnight train in the custody of Deputy U.S. Marshal Custis Long of the Denver Federal District.

Longarm, as he was better known to friend and foe alike, knew just how *he* felt about the fair grub and genuine Arbuckle coffee they'd be serving up ahead in the dining car most any time now. For they'd both missed dinner back yonder in Chicago Town the previous evening because of all the paperwork it took to transfer a convicted road agent with homicidal tendencies from one court's jurisdiction to a more serious one. And they both had slept past breakfast aboard the train that morning.

Longarm's pocket watch and the way the autumn sun was glaring down at the monotonous tawny prairie they were crossing were in total agreement that it was time for someone to be sounding the dining car chimes in the corridor outside their stuffy private compartment. Figuring on most any minute now, Longarm rose to his considerable height, even in low-heeled army boots, to see what he could do about his public image before exposing it to the snooty glances of the mostly greenhorn public a good old boy was likely to encounter on a train to Denver, which was getting

1

mighty fancy since they'd turned the old Cherry Creek gold fields into an official state capital.

Staring morosely at his lean, tanned self in that full-length mirror mounted on the compartment door, Longarm adjusted his limp shoestring tie. They'd made him wear it with a whole damned suit on official visits like this one ever since President Hayes and his Lemonade Lucy had made it to the White House with all those promises to tidy things up after the hell-for-leather Grant Administration.

The suit, of course, was a rough tobacco brown tweed that an active gent could act up in without it showing much. The free-swinging tails of the frock coat kept the Colt .44–40 he still had to pack, cross-draw, along with handcuffs and such, from disturbing dudes unduly in passing. He naturally kept his federal badge, identification, and back-up derringer completely out of sight until such times as he might have call to show them.

Few greenhorns noticed his spurless stovepipe boots under the cuffs of his snugly tailored pants. This far east, the broad-brimmed snuff-brown Stetson he wore telescoped in the High Plains style drew amused or confused glances now and again. But Longarm didn't care. Government regulations called for a hat and tie on duty in town. It didn't say what *sort* of hat.

Adjusting his Stetson cavalry-style, as if getting ready for an inspection by Miss Lemonade Lucy Hayes in the flesh, Longarm told his prisoner, "I ain't more anxious than yourself to get stared at in the dining car, old son. But this train won't get us into more discreet surroundings this side of sundown, Lord willing and the trestles all stay up. So there's two ways we can work her. Them handcuffs you have on won't attract too much notice if we put a flannel blanket over 'em from my possibles roll, as if you maybe had the ague and needed a lap robe whilst you eat."

"I ain't about to walk the length of this blamed train chained up like some wild beast!" the prisoner shouted, raising his cuffed wrists to shake both fists at Longarm. "I'd rather starve!"

To which Longarm firmly replied, although not unkindly, "Speak for yourself. I'm hungry as a bitch wolf, and you *were* a wild beast when you shot that schoolmarm as you tore out of the Castle Rock Post Office."

Tanner said, "Aw, I was only trying to scare folks. I swear I never aimed at that gal coming outten a shop across the way. First time I noticed she was in my line of fire was when she commenced to flop about on the walk!"

Longarm muttered dryly, "It's a caution how folks do that, once they've been gut-shot with a .45. But as I was saying before you reminded me why I'm taking you back to Colorado, there's two ways. Trail bedding ain't all I carry with me in my possibles roll when I figure to be out in the field overnight."

Stretching some, Longarm reached for the McClellan saddle he'd lashed earlier to the baggage rack above his own seat. "My boss, Marshal Billy Vail, makes me tote cruel and unusual punishments along whether I need to use 'em or not. I told you when I picked you up last night I'd as soon just gun any asshole dumb enough to run from me, next to hauling him about chained hand and foot. But fair is fair and you just said you didn't want to traipse up to the dining car with me of your own free will."

Blue Tooth Tanner eyed the massive, brutal leg-irons warily as Longarm turned to face him with them, explaining, "If I was to fit one of these around each of your ankles, with the chain back behind that steel end-brace of your seat, I'd say it would almost be safe to leave you alone in here for, oh, five minutes?"

The more casually dressed prisoner smiled sheepishly, exposing the bucktooth that had died and turned slate blue to give him his handle as he replied, "Five or even *six*, Boss. I don't suppose I could get you to bring me back some

3

bread and butter, once you've finished your noon dinner up forward?"

Longarm almost said something dumb. Then he reflected that his prisoner might not try so hard at first if he thought he had plenty of time. So he simply nodded and said he might even manage a ham on rye if Tanner would promise not to escape before he got back.

Blue Tooth did, for all that meant. So Longarm hunkered down to chain Tanner's booted ankles securely. Then, lest a gent on his way to a federal hanging bruise his fool self in thrashing about, Longarm removed one wrist cuff and snapped it back in place with the chain threaded under the armrest at that same end of the green plush seat. Blue Tooth bitched it was an uncomfortable way to ride. Longarm told him it wasn't half as uncomfortable as it could get in *any* position by sundown without a bite to eat all day. Then he rose, put a thoughtful hand on the door latch, and studied his securely chained prisoner to see what he might have done wrong.

He couldn't see anything. Besides, Blue Tooth Tanner had been dumb enough during the robbery to disguise his horse face with a small domino mask covering only his nondescript oyster gray *eyes*. So Longarm figured he didn't have much to worry about. He nodded, said something about being back in less than an hour, and ducked out into the narrow corridor running a third the length of that particular car.

There were close to a dozen other cars, coach or Pullman, this side of the forward diner. Longarm knew his prisoner knew that. So he only moved up to the wider space near the front of their car, where he could still keep an eye on the door to his compartment, as he fished out a three-for-a-nickel cheroot and lit it.

A million years and, say, two dozen drags of smoke later, a young colored gent in a white linen jacket came along the corridor with a forearm's worth of flat chimes, banging them fit to bust as he called out more softly that

4

they were fixing to start serving up ahead.

Longarm saw he hadn't been the only one aboard with a growling stomach as soon as other doors along the corridor commenced to slide open. A mighty fine young blonde in a tan poplin duster popped out of her own compartment to lead the stampede, passing Longarm before the colored gent with the gongs made it up to him.

Longarm didn't care about the hungry blonde. He stopped the dining car crewman with a friendly smile and bet him four bits a lawman transporting a prisoner couldn't get served back here in a private compartment.

He lost, of course, and decided it was worth it when the easygoing colored gent produced a menu out of thin air and said he'd be back to take their order once he got done donging the others forward to dine the usual way.

There sure were a heap of them, male, female, handsome, not so handsome, and downright ugly. More than one old boy and at least two women who passed Longarm were dressed more ragged-ass than old Blue Tooth inside. None seemed to have any trouble easing by as Longarm stood his ground in that wider but far from spacious end of the corridor. Then a sort of gorilla or grizzly sporting a checked vest, white Texas hat, and Walker .45 conversion strode dead-center down on Longarm to grumble, "You're blocking my way, pilgrim."

Longarm was already leaning his back against the bulkhead. So he couldn't back up any farther, and said so in as amiable a tone as the situation called for. He'd already decided that while most Texicans wore their hats crowned tall to keep their scalps a shade cooler under their more ferocious sun, this one had his hat crowned even taller to *look* ferocious, which hardly seemed fair since the asshole stood close to seven feet tall in his high-heeled border boots to begin with.

The big man in the big hat placed a thoughtful palm on the grips of his big gun as he repeated, "I'm trying to get

5

through here whilst you block egress with that sissy see-gar, sonny."

Longarm blew some smoke in the bully's beefy face before he quietly said, "Don't fuck with me. I mean it."

The big Texican reared back on his high heels to demand, "Who do you think you are and who do you think you're talking to so suicidal, little darling?"

So Longarm had the muzzle of his own .44–40 imbedded deep in the bully's beefy gut by the time he softly replied, "Let's just say I'm as harmless a cuss as you'd *let* me be, if you had a lick of sense, you loud-talking and slow-drawing bastard!"

The stranger, now sort of ashen-faced, allowed that since Longarm was putting it *that* way, he'd just as soon mosey on up to the old dining car and see what they were serving for dinner.

Another million years went by while Longarm memorized that menu and searched his memory for the ugly face that went with that handsome ten-gallon hat. By the time the colored dining-car gonger got back to him he'd decided that fried ham and hash browns might be safer than anything off the steam table after fifteen hours out along the rails. He'd also decided that he'd never seen that swaggering Texican before.

He told the colored gent to just forget the deep-fried greens they offered with the ham, and asked if they could have some extra coffee with their apple pie instead.

The gong-wrangler said that part would be easy, but warned Longarm there might be a wait, since the car up ahead would be full of earlier famine victims and only one of the cooks really had four arms. So Longarm told him to take his own good time because waiting for a meal passed time aboard a train almost as good as eating it slow could.

After they'd parted friendly Longarm settled back against the bulkhead to smoke and stare through the glass across the corridor some more. He knew the passing scenery would be just as tedious from their compartment windows, and if he waited in there he'd have to unchain his prisoner, lest he seem downright chickenshit.

Putting those leg-irons away again seemed only decent, as long as things up forward went as planned. But he knew that the best-laid plans of mice and men could turn out unexpectedly, and if he had to track down their noon dinners in the sweet by and by, his prisoner would say something mean about him acting nervous with those leg-irons again.

But what the hell, time passed as slow or fast out here in the corridor, and it wasn't as if a man had to rest a good pair of legs after spending the better part of the trip on his ass.

He didn't have to tell himself the true reason he preferred his own company out here was the iota of sympathy he'd caught himself feeling for the poor brainless boob he was transporting back to Denver for that doubtless-overdue rope dance.

It wasn't going to take them long, once old Blue Tooth Tanner had been handed over to the hangman's tender mercies. For the not-too-bright *bandito* had already stood trial in federal court in Denver for killing that schoolmarm in the process of robbing a U.S. post office. Old Judge Dickerson had naturally sentenced Tanner to death for his misdeeds in Colorado. But then Illinois had asked if they could tidy up their own books by trying him on earlier charges stemming from his salad days in the Chicago stockyards. Judge Dickerson, being a sport, had said it was jake with him as long as *somebody* hung the son of a bitch.

Illinois had tried. But in the end all they'd nailed Tanner on was armed robbery and bestiality with a lamb that his lawyers had insisted he'd saved from a worser fate. So after some wires back and forth it had been agreed their best bet would be to hang him back in Colorado for the slaughter of that schoolmarm in Castle Rock, and where was that confounded dining-car gonger with the damned old grub?

7

Longarm finished another cheroot in vain, only to see even more famine victims traipsing forward to hog all the grub. Longarm was tempted to just go back inside and wait sitting down. But he doubted it would be more comfortable with a growling gut and a condemned man for company. So he stood pat and waited another million years, staring out at mile after mile of mighty-wide-open nothingness.

The High Plains would begin to roll more interestingly later in the day as they approached the Front Range you could admire from downtown Denver. But this far east the prairie lay as flat and dull as an awesomely big doormat from horizon to horizon, and when it was dry, like today, the sky could get mighty dull to look at as well. They called this stretch the Big Lonely, and the monotonous-looking homestead gals along the way were in the habit of slashing their own throats with monotonous regularity.

He told himself not to study on that homestead gal he'd found all aswarm with blowfly maggots once, not with greasy ham and hash browns due to come his way anytime now.

After riding through a war or more and serving with the Justice Department six or eight years, one might expect a man to pay less heed to the sweet and sour breath of Mister Death. But while not a sentimental sissy when it came to outlaws and other varmints, Longarm seldom enjoyed killing and tended to hold his fire when it was at all practical.

He knew it wouldn't be practical to spare Blue Tooth Tanner's miserable neck, of course. For whether the simple bastard had killed with malice or by accident, as he claimed, the rest of the human race couldn't afford to let such a dangerous animal live. But it seemed just as well to Longarm, after getting to know the old boy for just one morning, that somebody else would be stuck with the chore of executing him.

Newspaper reporters and other folks who didn't have to tidy up after killers tended to consider hangmen cold unfeeling butchers because they handled their chores with such swift and sometimes brutal effectiveness. But Longarm had bellied up to many a bar, afterwards, with such notorious hangmen as old George Maledon of Fort Smith, who'd likely hung more poor bastards than anyone. Old George and all the others, save for a few mean-hearted bastards, agreed that the meanest way to hang a man was to draw the process out with mock kindness, urging him to say just a few last words and giving him plenty of time to choke back sobs and piss his pants, instead of just frog-marching him up those thirteen steps to have the halter around his neck and the trap sprung under him before he felt dead certain he was really done for.

Longarm swore at himself for dwelling on matters that he couldn't do enough about to matter. Despite how long it felt just waiting, Longarm was a good enough judge of true time to wonder how that pretty blonde could have ordered and eaten so soon when she suddenly popped back through the front doorway of the car, her face flushed and more than one hair out of place.

He wondered even more when she suddenly swung belly to belly with him, as if she wanted to kiss him, save for the expression of total dismay on her pretty face.

Then Longarm saw the big male paw that had gripped her by one arm of her duster and swung her into such a mutually awkward fix. So as the burly Texican who went with the big fist followed it the rest of the way into view, Longarm quietly asked the lady if she was arm in arm with that other gent of her own free will.

Before the blonde could reply, the cuss in the ten-gallon hat growled, "I'd keep my own nose under the brim of my own High Plains hat if I was you, little darling."

To which Longarm could only reply in dulcet tones, "It may be just as well I ain't you then. I was speaking to this here lady and if I *was* you, I'd commence by letting go her arm."

The bully did no such thing as he protested, "See here, I just now set across from her polite and offered to pay for her

9

dining-car meal, friendly as anything. But she just throwed down her fool napkin, sprang skywards as if I'd spilt hot coffee in her lap, and flounced out as if I'd done something wrong. Since then I've followed her the whole length of this whole train demanding some answer to her insulting behavior, and as you see, she *still* won't talk to *either* of us'n!"

Longarm said, "Let go her arm and mayhaps I can explain some of the rules of polite train travel, Tex."

When nothing happened he added, an octave lower, "Let go her arm. I mean it."

The bully in the checked vest and Walker Conversion didn't seem to think Longarm meant it. He still hung on—with his gun hand, the asshole—while the bewildered-looking blonde told one or the other of them, *"Ich verstehe nicht! Ich spreche kaum Englisch!"*

So Longarm simply threw a left cross over her shoulder to sucker-punch the moron holding on to her, and sure enough, he let go of her arm as his head thudded back into a doorpost. He then proceeded to slide slowly down.

The foreign gal was halfway to her own compartment door by the time her molester made it all the way to the flooring. And so Longarm felt no need to kick a man who was down as the maiden who was no longer in distress called something that sounded like donkey chimes before ducking safely inside her own compartment.

The Texican who'd been pestering her had lost his big white hat sliding down the doorpost. As he sat there in one corner, glassy-eyed and bleeding a bit out of one corner of his big mouth, Longarm hunkered down to gather up the fallen hat and brush it with one tweedy elbow as he amiably explained, "Aside from being a lady dining alone, the gal was a foreigner who just couldn't say what she thought of you in any lingo you could follow. I suspicion that was High Dutch she was just spouting."

"You son of a bitch! You cold-cocked me!" the man he'd cold-cocked shouted as his befuddled brain started ticking again.

10

Longarm held the hat out to him, saying, "Yeah. Like I was just saying, your doubtless-well-meant attentions spooked that sort of high-toned little lady considerably, and I might have done both of you a favor by breaking it up before anyone could get all excited and cable Der Kaiser about international incidents. I recall this time, down Mexico way, when this high-toned lady who spoke neither Anglo nor Mex—"

"You cold-cocked me in front of a woman, and now I'm going to have to kill you total!" the brute he'd belted cut in, trying to get up and go for his own gun at the same time.

So this time Longarm didn't pull his punch, and after a while another passenger came back from the dining car and offered to fetch the conductor when Longarm flashed his badge and sort of explained.

The conductor joined Longarm and his stretched-out victim a few minutes later. He agreed Longarm had done what had only been right, but when Longarm suggested they just roll the surly cuss off at the next water stop, the conductor explained how awkward that could be for a mere senior employee.

The asshole Longarm had just knocked out, twice, was a major holder of Chicago, Burlington & Quincy stock and a mighty mogul of the beef industry. When Longarm pointed out he'd been acting more like a drunken drag rider in a Dodge City whorehouse the conductor agreed he was notorious for that as well.

In the end they decided it might be best to just stuff the big pest in his own compartment, minus his gunbelt, and allow him to come to such senses as he had in his own good time. So that was what the conductor and one of his porters did in the end, with the conductor hanging on to the Walker Conversion for now. When he pointed out he'd have to return the asshole's property as soon as they got to the end of the line, Longarm agreed that would only be right, and suggested a good nap followed by a pounding headache would likely calm the cuss by sundown.

A few more passengers came by. Then that colored ding-donger got back to Longarm's car with plenty of grub and joe on a good-sized tray with skinny fold-down legs one could use to convert it to a piss-poor table. So Longarm tipped him an extra dime just to set it up inside between the facing seats.

After he'd left, Longarm left Blue Tooth Tanner's leg-irons on so he could eat with total ease without handcuffs. For a man who'd said he wasn't hungry, old Blue Tooth sure tore into his ham and hash browns. When Longarm said so, the doomed outlaw sighed and said, "The spirit is willing but the flesh is weak. I've been trying like anything to go easy on the grub since they said you was coming to fetch me for the hangman, but to tell the truth I just can't seem to refuse anything worth eating or drinking."

Longarm washed some chewed ham down with Arbuckle and asked how come, adding, "Ain't it a mite late to worry about your figure or even your health, no offense?"

Tanner confided, "I was there when they hung my poor old daddy. Some others who was there laughed when he shit himself so much at the end. Daddy had ordered himself a swell last meal, and you could smell the oysters and fancy fish sauce he'd et the night before as he dangled there in the cold gray light of dawn."

Longarm swallowed ham that had suddenly gone awfully greasy as he refrained from commenting on the results of feeding a whole regiment a swell supper of pork sausages and sauerkraut the evening before a serious battle in a summer rain. It hardly seemed a fine topic to discuss across a dinner table. So when Blue Tooth Tanner wistfully asked whether a hanged man shit himself worth mentioning on an empty stomach, Longarm assured him he'd seen lots of old boys dangle dry and dignified.

It wasn't true, but he didn't see how his prisoner was going to know for sure before it would hardly matter, to him, so what the hell, it seemed the least he could do.

Blue Tooth cast all caution aside as he enjoyed the apple pie and mousetrap cheese with extra sugar in his genuine Arbuckle Brand. He said he felt sure he'd have time to go back on a diet between the time Longarm handed him over in Denver and the time they actually hung him.

Longarm didn't answer. Tanner would learn soon enough that they meant to drop him through the trap on arrival to save the expenses of making up and cleaning out an extra cell at the Federal House of Detention close by the railroad yards. When old Judge Dickerson sentenced a cuss he paid attention to the fine print, and there was seldom if ever any bullshit with appeals and stays of execution, but Longarm had no call to crush a prisoner's hopes. So he never did, unless the cuss had done someone Longarm knew real dirty.

Longarm wouldn't have known that schoolmarm in Castle Rock had he woke up in bed with her, dead or alive, and Blue Tooth had said he hadn't meant it personally. So Longarm just let the poor doomed rascal dream of hanging in the sweet by and by as they rolled ever closer to the waiting gallows with every clickety-clack of the steel wheels under them. So, dull as this run across the sunbaked prairie usually was, it seemed no time at all before that helpful colored gent had cleared away their repast around three or four in the afternoon and returned with the beer schooners Longarm had asked him to fetch for them from the club car.

Blue Tooth Tanner, back in handcuffs but out of his leg-irons again by that time, allowed Longarm was a real sport to serve beer to a prisoner like that. But Longarm just shrugged and told him he was lucky he wasn't an Indian. He didn't trust Blue Tooth enough to confide he often drank with Indians, no matter what Miss Lemonade Lucy had to say about that.

Blue Tooth would have liked it, but Longarm didn't order them any more beer after that colored gent came for the schooners around Longarm's usual quitting time. He told

13

them they weren't fixing to serve supper at the usual time because the train would be rolling into Denver, at the end of the line, about the time when most of the folks would be starting their main entrée. Longarm tipped him another nickel and told him there was no call to worry further about their comforts.

As if even feeble minds could run in the same channels, Tanner suddenly blurted out, "I can't believe we're getting there this soon! I mean they told me it would take till sundown, and I was sort of anxious to savor as much more of the Lord's Good Earth as I could before they shut my eyes on me forever, but there's so much of it *left* out yonder for a man to see, and this fool train is going so blamed *fast!*"

Longarm lit two cheroots and handed one across to Tanner as he soberly said, "I know. I'm sorry this last trip you'd get to take had to be so sun-bleached and drab, old son, but they weren't holding you for us near Niagara Falls or the Painted Desert."

Tanner almost sobbed, "I'd like to see a lot more of all that swell shortgrass and that clear blue sky out yonder! I swear I'd take it in the ass and swallow the contents of a whole spittoon for just one day, one lousy *day,* walking free across all that dry and dusty downright beautiful open range!"

Longarm didn't doubt him. It would have been needlessly cruel to point out it had been the fool's own grand design to forsake a life on the open range as a poor but honest rider for the shorter excitement of the owlhoot trail. He knew Tanner had doubtless come to that very same conclusion by now.

So they smoked and jawed some more, with Longarm steering the conversation to such cheerful topics as the poor cuss knew about, until sure enough, as the range outside was starting to roll ever more and turn ever more golden in the gloaming light, they began to pass low-slung home spreads, herds of beef gathered about the tanks of sunflower windmills for their bedtime waterings and so forth. Tanner said it had always made him feel sort of sad when the sun was setting, even when he had no reason. He said it got far worse when a man commenced to count how many sunsets he might ever see. When he asked Longarm how many days it usually took them to hang a man where they were going, Longarm said he didn't know and then, when pressed, made a guess at six weeks or so. They'd told him, growing up in West-by-God-Virginia, that a white lie was seldom entered in Saint Peter's book against a sinner.

So it was almost dark, that tricky twilight Longarm didn't like for gunfighting, when they rolled at last into Denver. He wasn't expecting anyone to be laying for him with a gun at the Union Depot, though. So he just told Blue Tooth to wait a spell as he got down his McClellan, explaining it was less awkward to get a prisoner and heavy-laden saddle off a train after most of the others had gotten off.

Blue Tooth Tanner said he was in no hurry. So they finished a brace of cheroots they'd been smoking before Longarm decided they might as well get cracking.

It worked. There was nobody in the corridor and nobody got in their way as Longarm led Tanner off, handcuffed to his own left wrist with the McClellan braced on his right hip. Longarm wasn't too pleased to see that nobody from his department seemed to be there to meet them. He muttered, "That'll learn me to roll into town at supper time. Let's drift down to the end of this platform and cut the smart way out of here, old son. Every fool in Creation will be out front by the carriage stands, cluttering the walk, and we don't need a ride, as far as we have to go."

Blue Tooth tagged along, gazing about at surroundings he found as unfamiliar as a kid at a county fair, while Longarm peered ahead through the tricky light for the baggage-way through dark brick walls that would shortcut them out to Wynkoop Street. So it was Blue Tooth, not Longarm, who suddenly gasped, "Jesus! Down!" and dragged Longarm after him to the cement as a gun muzzle flamed from the blackness to their left to fill the gloomy train shed with

15

roaring echoes and spanging lead!

Longarm heaved the heavy saddle between their prone forms and the source of all that gunfire, for all the good even thick saddle leather might do, as he somehow got his own gun out from between his left hip and Tanner's right one. Then he was firing back at a vicious fool who insisted on blazing round after round from the same stand, inky black or not, until, sure enough, they heard the murderous asshole wail, "Oh, Mamma, your boy's been hurt real bad!"

Even fools who fired more than once from the same stand could fib to a foeman. So Longarm lobbed another couple of rounds into that voice, closer to his own level, and heard it wail, "Oh, no! Don't punish me no more and I'll be good!"

A more familiar voice called out behind Longarm, claiming to be Sergeant Nolan of the Denver P.D. and demanding to know what all that noise was about.

Longarm called back, "I wish I knew, Nolan. I'd be Long, out of Justice, pinned down over here with a prisoner I just got off that Burlington train with. I might have hit our surly welcoming committee, but you never know, so keep your head down till we can get us some light on the subject!"

Nolan didn't work for Longarm, so once he'd issued orders of his own he joined the two of them on the cement behind the saddle, saying, "I sent my boys to fetch some bull's-eye lanterns. Do you reckon they were out to free this other bastard here?"

Longarm shook his head and replied, "Tanner ain't exactly what I'd call a bastard, Sarge. He's a convicted killer, I'll allow, but he just now saved my bacon by spotting an ambush I was too dumb to see."

Nolan said in that case he'd shake with a man who'd just saved the man he owed his own stripes to. Longarm said he'd rather Nolan keep an eye on Tanner as he moved in on that other shootist. So Nolan said he'd be proud to, and after some belly-down awkwardness Longarm had himself uncuffed. He reloaded and holstered his side arm, and slipped his sixteen-shot Winchester from its saddle boot to do some serious hunting.

He rolled well clear of their meager cover in dead silence, and rose as quietly to cross the tracks and platform beyond in a low running crouch. He saw why nobody was shooting at him when he got to the blurred form sprawled on the cinders of the track bed beyond. There was just enough light to make out the checked vest. The big white hat was upside down a couple of cross-ties away. Longarm dropped down there with him and kicked that Walker Conversion clean out of sight before, his Winchester across his own thighs, he said not unkindly, "I was wondering how come you seemed to be more scared than hurt by those last pistol rounds. Where did I hull you before you dropped, and whatever possessed a grown man to behave so foolish?"

"He shamed me, Mamma," the bully sort of croaked, adding in an even softer gurgle, "The gal was too stuck up to play with me, like that Sally Anne who sneered at us and wouldn't invite me to her birthday doings that time. I was fixing to show her, like I showed that Sally Anne out back in our alley, only this bigger boy horned in and hit me, right in front of Sally Anne!"

Longarm sensed light and movement and got up to see a Denver copper badge coming their way with a bull's-eye lantern. Longarm directed the other lawman to shine the wan beam on the wealthy cattle baron who'd been sent back to what sounded like a sort of deprived childhood. They both saw the poor bastard would never be worried about old age. The copper badge whistled softly and declared, "Smack through his rib cage, twice. Lord only knows how come he's still breathing. Who was he, Longarm?"

The dying man at their feet declared, "My mamma may take in washing since my daddy fell off in that stampede, but someday I'll be big as any of you and then I'll show you!"

Longarm quietly suggested, "The railroad will have his name for us. He was a mucky-muck from out Chicago way traveling in his own private compartment, and like you just heard him say, he was out to show us."

Sergeant Nolan joined them, hauling Longarm's saddle and Tanner along. Longarm told them all, "I had words with him on the train this afternoon and let that be a lesson to us all. I thought we were only arguing about a gal. He seems to have taken it as some sort of mortal insult to his family honor."

The man at their feet groaned, "Please make it stop, Mamma! I paid them back for low-rating your red hands and no proper hat to wear in church. But now I'm feeling mighty poorly and I wish I could have some of that medicine you take all the time for your troubles."

Then they heard a dreadful gasp, followed by an heroic farting, and then nothing at all as Blue Tooth Tanner sighed and said, "I wish he hadn't reminded me. How soon did you say it might take to have *me* flapping like a fish and shitting like a fool at the end of the hangman's line, Longarm?"

Once he'd nudged the cadaver with a boot tip to make dead sure Longarm soberly replied, "Not as soon as they might have planned. They say this was a cattle baron I just had to gun, and it's been quite a spell since you could even gun a hobo within the city limits of a state capital without explaining your reasons to a coroner's jury. So aside from feeling much obliged, I'm going to have to call you as my only witness to a shoot-out in self-defense, Mister Tanner."

His prisoner gasped and swayed in weak relief as he asked in a tone of laconic desperation, "Are you saying they might let me off with Life at Hard if you was to tell 'em how I just saved you?"

Longarm just felt sort of sick as he assured Tanner he meant to put that down in writing. It would have been needlessly unkind to hazard even a guess as to how long a stay of execution they might be talking about.

Chapter 2

It was far shorter stay than Longarm had expected, and he was used to the ways of the fair but firm Judge Dickerson. It might have taken longer back in the days of the Pony Express and mail coaches. But thanks to modern wonders of wet-cell electricity and the help of both Western Union and the railroads involved, it was soon established that the late W. R. Callisher of ten-gallon and .45-caliber notoriety had been as noted for his nasty temper as he had for his railroad stock and beef herd.

Even better for Longarm, the railroad wired in depositions from that conductor and more than one of his train crew regarding Callisher's oafish behavior aboard that train as well as the nice way Longarm had tried to deal with him.

The coroner's jury was pleased to take Blue Tooth Tanner's more direct testimony involving events taking place shortly before and after he'd spied a white hat in the gloom of that train shed and instinctively recognized the intent behind its sudden movement as Callisher dropped into a gunfighting crouch. But the real clincher was the deposition from the Prussian Consulate, translated into English and signed by a Frau Erica Von Lowendorf, who praised the actions of the obvious *Amerikanisch* aristocrat who'd saved her from the unwelcome attentions of an obvious

19

Amerikanisch peasant as she was on her way to join her husband, the military attaché at Fort Bliss, Texas. So Longarm could have had himself decorated by Der Kaiser if he'd wanted to traipse all the way to Berlin Town. Everyone closer to home allowed he'd done 'em proud and only done what was right by a homicidal pest.

So the morning after he got that in writing Longarm made a point of getting to his office in the Denver Federal Building early.

This seemed to shock young Henry, who played the typewriter and warned visitors in the reception room that they needed some sensible reason, if not an appointment, to see the one and original U.S. Marshal William Vail, hiding out in the back.

Longarm didn't need an appointment, since he worked there, but he'd still learned to ask the pasty-faced Henry whether the boss was in alone before he barged back to the office.

When he asked that morning, Henry nodded but asked, "What happened? Were you unlucky at cards or does she hanker for more than the usual flowers, books, and candy? We just got paid last week and we put you in for all three trips you made last month at six to twelve a mile, so—"

"I ain't scouting for an advance on next month, Henry," Longarm cut in, moving on by without elaboration lest the fool kid think him a sentimental fool.

He found their superior, known to his pals as Billy Vail, in a better than average mood in his oak-paneled office, which could have used a good airing. The older, shorter, and far stouter marshal insisted on smoking pungent fat cigars with all the windows closed against the thin crisp autumn air of the Mile High City.

As Longarm sat uninvited in the one decent leather-covered chair on his own side of the older lawman's cluttered desk, Vail shot a glance at the banjo clock on one oak wall. "You can't leave early for that harvest festival at the Grange Hall. I know she's pretty and that you ain't had any

20

with her yet. My wife tells me all the gossip. But we still give the taxpayers a full day's work in this damned outfit, you horny cuss."

Longarm got out a cheroot of his own in self-defense, smiled sort of sheepishly, and refrained from allowing that the gossip about that particular pretty neighbor was a tad behind the times. For any man who boasted about his screwing would likely brag about his other body functions as well.

After lighting his own smoke, Longarm quietly said, "I was just down the hall talking to Judge Dickerson's clerk. You drink personally with the judge himself, don't you, Billy?"

Vail nodded. "All right, you can knock off at five if you just have to. I already asked. The answer is no. Tanner's been found guilty of Homicide in the First and sentenced to hang by the neck until dead, dead, dead. Period."

Longarm blew a thoughtful smoke ring and declared, "Billy, I was walking into it like a big bird with blinkers on. Callisher was after me, not my prisoner. If Blue Tooth had just done nothing at all I'd have likely wound up dead with him still alive and free to help himself to my handcuff key, my money, and my gun."

Vail blew a thicker, more pungent donut and simply replied in a card-dealing tone, "He could have. But he didn't. One's inclined to doubt he'd have gunned that innocent bystander, that schoolmarm down to Castle Rock, if he'd been born with the ability to plan ahead on short notice. He spotted hostile intent and sounded a warning by instinct, the way a yard dog might have. You don't owe him any more than that, old son."

Longarm nodded soberly but said, "I'd hardly hang a yard dog, even a biter, for warning me just in time there was a weasel in my henhouse."

Vail shrugged. "Neither would I. But Tanner wasn't found guilty of being a mean yard dog by a jury of his peers. He owes a life for a life, and his saving *your* life

21

don't cut no ice with Judge Dickerson, or the kith and kin of that innocent young schoolmarm he gut-shot down in Castle Rock for no better reason!"

Longarm started to protest, then sighed and allowed, "I reckon there's no sensible answer to your draconian words of wisdom. But there sure are days I don't enjoy this job. Old Blue Tooth's sent word he'd like for me to come by and visit with him some more in the time he has left. I've already done that more than once. I've brought him tobacco, sweets, and some books before I found out he can't read. I know what he's going to ask me and I know I'm just going to wind up saying I'll try some more."

Billy Vail nodded soberly and said, "I've had to stand by as they hung someone I wasn't really sore at in my time. It can go with this job when the job's done proper and impartial. We know you've done all you can for the poor dumb cuss. So if I was you I wouldn't go to see him any more."

Longarm shrugged, flicked ash on the carpet to keep down any carpet mites, and muttered, "You ain't me. Before I had time to think I sent back word I'd come by some more, unless I got called out of town."

Vail shrugged and suggested, "There you go then. Just stay the hell away from the gloomy cuss and let him think you've been sent somewhere else."

To which Longarm replied, "*Bueno*. Where are you sending me, to do what?"

Vail blinked, laughed incredulously, and started to tell his senior deputy not to ask such silly questions. But he could see Longarm really meant it. That was one of the problems you could have with a man who took pride in keeping his word.

Vail muttered, "Thunderation, we don't have any outstanding warrants that could carry you far enough to matter. I take it you'd as soon be out in the field when they swing old Blue Tooth next week?"

Longarm grumbled, "Yep. Damned hangman sure picked a swell time for his damned daughter's wedding. I make it eight or ten days before I can rest more easy about a shiftless skunk I owe."

Vail hesitated, then began to rummage through the disorganized papers on his desk. "I did have a dumb request from the B.I.A. here somewhere, speaking of shiftless skunks. They asked for you by name. You'd think by now they'd have all the damned sign-talking scouts they'd ever need, and I was fixing to have Henry type up a letter to turn them down."

Longarm frowned thoughtfully and said, "I ain't scouted all that much, and your average Indian agent knows as much or more sign as I do, Billy."

Vail said, "I was just going to have Henry point that out to them. I suspect they only asked for you by name because they know you scouted Shoshoni for the cavalry that time in '78 when Buffalo Horn rose up by the South Pass."

Longarm said, "Buffalo Horn and his young men were more Bannock than true Shoshoni, if you want to put a fine point on it, and as I recall with some dismay, the army shot the shit out of Buffalo Horn's band, including Buffalo Horn, and then shot a mess of mighty surprised Shoshoni for dessert before those of us who knew better could stop 'em."

Vail nodded. "The B.I.A. noticed. You've got quite a rep for getting along tolerably with Mister Lo, the Poor Indian. So anyway, they wanted to know if they could borrow you some more for some delicate negotiating with the Lemhi Shoshoni over by their Snake River."

Longarm said, "They call themselves Agaidukas if we're talking about the so-called Shoshoni and Bannock under old Chief Pocatello on the Fort Hall Reservation. Lemhi Shoshoni, or Western Snakes, was bestowed on 'em by mountain men, Mormon settlers, and such."

Vail sighed wearily and muttered, "Jesus H. Christ, if I ask the kid what time it might be he tells me how to build a clock! I just now told you the B.I.A. admired your astounding grasp of Indian lore. Do you want to mosey over to Fort Hall and see what's eating those damned Indians by any name or don't you?"

Longarm said, "I do. Anything beats staying in Denver for that infernal hanging."

Vail shrugged. "Oh, I don't know. Nobody said a thing about hanging *you,* and they do say Shoshoni squaws like to broil a captive's dick on a stick, with him still connected to it."

Chapter 3

The rest of the morning was more tedious than torturous for a man who was anxious to get out of town. Billy Vail told Henry to get in touch with Interior and make sure they understood Justice was paying no field expenses for such tomfoolery. Then he told Longarm that even if he wanted to ride with the party headed out west to powwow with Pocatello, it would be best to wait until the dudes got considerably closer.

They'd be expecting to meet Longarm and some Mormon scouts at Ogden, in Utah Territory, where everyone had to switch from rail to mule trains for the rough going up into the Indian country that Little Big Eyes, or Secretary of the Interior Carl Schurz, aimed to buy from his red children for his white children. The bargain-hunters were likely crossing the Mississippi about now, and anyway, nobody Blue Tooth was likely to send after Longarm with yet another plaintive invite was likely to know where to find him after quitting time.

He read the little Henry had given him about the request from the B.I.A. at the bar of the nearby Parthenon Saloon, and put the carbon copies away when he was joined by Crawford, a reporter for the *Denver Post,* who quietly observed, "I figured you might be in here. At the risk of spoiling a good story, I feel I have to warn a pal I'm not the only one looking for you this afternoon. He's about your height and my build, wearing an undertaker's expression as well as an outfit picked out for him by the late Edgar Allan Poe. When last seen inquiring for you over in the Black Cat he had on a black Texas hat and low-slung *buscadero* gun rig as well. Would you like to make a statement for the *Post* whilst there's time?"

Longarm washed down the rest of the pickled pig's knuckle he'd been working on with some needled beer before he replied. "Sounds like another lawman or a hired gun. A Texas Ranger new in town might not have heard about my disagreement with that barmaid at the Black Cat. I shot the only Texican really mad at me last week. But like the old song says, farther along we'll know more about it. Anyone who told him I sometimes lunched in the Black Cat would have surely mentioned this place as well."

Crawford moved out of the line of fire between Longarm and the nearby swinging doors as Longarm simply let his loose frock coat hang free of his gun grips while he shifted his beer schooner to his left fist, asking, "Might you have much on Chief Pocatello of the Western Shoshoni in your back files, pard?"

The shorter but thicker-set newspaper man blinked owlishly and volunteered, "Bad Injun in his day. He and his Snakes got to count coup on a couple of dozen troopers and Lord knows how many wagon trains during the Civil War. General Connor and his Nevada Volunteers caught up with him and his band on the Overland Trail near the end of the war, and would have hanged 'em the way they hanged all those Santee Sioux about the same time. But then old President Lincoln spoiled the fun with blanket pardons for the treacherous red devils, subject only to modest improvements in their manners."

Longarm grimaced and said, "Old Abe must have been on to something. They do say Pocatello's kept his word after making his mark on the Box Elder Treaty of '63, tempted as he might have been by the famine of '65 and the big Shoshoni Scare of '78. So what might I be missing about this deal?"

Not knowing what he was talking about, Crawford had no more to offer and said so. Longarm finished his beer, watching that doorway, as he idly wondered whether the back files of Crawford's paper could have such a simplistic view of Mister Lo.

He put his empty beer schooner down, having decided he'd just as soon risk a slap in the face as paper cuts on dusty fingers. He didn't tell Crawford just where he was headed, so the fool reporter wanted to tag along, lest he miss a front-page gunfight.

Longarm laughed sincerely and declared, "A gunfight was the last thing I had in mind, old son. That mysterious cuss with his hat crowned Texas-style is likely from the B.I.A. And he's likely as anxious as me to hear why in thunder even a sissy would need scouts, or even translators, to visit friendlies on a fully staffed agency."

"What if he's not? What if he's looking to fight you?" Crawford demanded hopefully.

Longarm snorted wryly and declared, "I reckon I'll fight him. Like I said, we'll know all about it farther along. Meanwhile, I eat my apples one bite at a time, and so now I'm off to see if someone who knows more than either of us about Indians can hazard a guess as to why I seem headed for Idaho Territory, Lord willing and the tracks don't wash out."

He got rid of the pesky reporter—it wasn't easy—and ducked through the big bottom floor of the Denver Dry Goods to make sure he wasn't being followed before he legged it on over to the terraced slopes of Capitol Hill.

He cut across the State House lawn, watching out for fresh sheep shit on the close-cropped leaf-littered buffalo grass as he tried to watch out for a possible ambush at the same time.

All the windows of the big stone State House were down, so it seemed safe not to worry about the afternoon sunlight

27

bouncing back his way from all that damned glass, while the cluster of folks he saw gathered around one of the cannons guarding the capitol steps didn't seem to be loading it up to fire on anyone. Colorado kept those big guns her volunteers had carried west from the war shined bright as gold, and tourists were always admiring hell out of them.

Passing safely by the cannon's mouth and glancing back as he crossed over to the state museum beyond, Longarm saw he didn't have anyone following him wearing any sort of hat. So he swung a tad wide of the regular entrance steps to enter by way of a more humble basement service door. Then he scouted up a side door barred to the general public and saying so, in gilt letters. He opened it and, as he'd hoped he might, caught Doctor Alexandria Henderson with a naked Indian.

The naked Indian on the deal table between them was one of those mummified cliff dwellers prospectors kept bringing back from the other side of Durango, and on second glance, old Sandy was really working on the baked clay pots they'd likely buried the cliff dweller with. Nobody knew why. The folks called Anasazi in Nadene, or Hohokam in Ho, had all been dried like figs before the first white folks, or even modern red ones, had shown up in the canyonlands to the southwest.

Sandy Henderson was a modern redhead with a passion to match on the rare occasions she let a man see her with all that red hair down and the rest of her out of that clean but spotted denim smock. Her lab smelled of fish glue at the moment and before Longarm could ask how come, the pretty little thing flashed her big aquamarine eyes at him warningly to declare, "Don't you dare come around on this side, and leave that door open behind you, Custis Long! I'm having enough trouble with this new pottery style, and even if I wasn't I'd be awfully cross with you!"

He left the door open, since she'd asked, and if it riled her it would serve her right. He ticked his hat brim at her and tried to sound serious as your average deacon as he said, "I don't blame you a bit, Miss Sandy. I told you last summer I was a tumbleweed cuss with an uncertain future. I'm here today on a mission for the U.S. Government."

To which she replied with an involuntary blush, "That's what you said the last time, and by the way it was last springtime, not last summer. You told me you wanted me to examine a Pawnee shield cover and the next thing I knew you were . . . examining *me* on top of that very shield cover, and . . . By the way, was I right about it being Pawnee workmanship?"

He had to smile, although politely, as he nodded and assured her they'd both guessed right that time. So she asked, "What have you got to show me this time, and I swear I'll scream if you take it out with that damned door wide open!"

He shut the door behind him with a boot heel, saying, "Life's too short to spend it arguing with ladies. I didn't bring any Indian stuff with me this time, Miss Sandy. I came to pick your brains about folks who mostly call themselves Ho. I got to go over by the Fort Hall Agency with some B.I.A. gents who seem more worried than the rest of us about the Indians they'll be meeting up with. As I understand it, they got a mixed bag of what Washington describes as Bannock and Shoshoni living at Fort Hall under Chief Pocatello."

Sandy nodded and said, "White Feather. He's all right. Probably smarter than Red Cloud and certainly smarter than Sitting Bull when it comes to dealing with the Bureau of Indian Affairs."

He nodded and said, "Old Washakie, The Rattle, seems to have his Wind River Shoshoni under control, east of the divide. But they say he was mighty vexed when the B.I.A. shoved a whole heap of Northern Arapaho down his throat, or leastways, on his reservation."

Sandy agreed Indian Affairs was in the habit of mixing oil and water. When she asked what events at Fort Washakie might have to do with his mission to Fort Hall, he explained, "Pocatello seems to have been put in charge of some leftover Bannock as well as his closer kin. I was wondering whether the Bannock know that, and as long as we're on the subject, would someone please tell me how to tell a Bannock from a Shoshoni?"

He risked edging around the dead cliff dweller for a clearer view of her skilled and pretty fingers as he added, "I mean, I have swapped shots and smoked weeds with both breeds and I'll milk a diamondback bare-handed if I can see any difference. They both hunt and fight on painted ponies. They both speak the same lingo, admire the same spirits, and describe themselves by the same sort of snaky wiggle in sign talk."

Sandy sighed and explained, "It's not them, it's us. The white Easterners who run the Bureau of Indian Affairs split the Western Shoshoni into two nations because some bands boiled their vegetables and some preferred to bake them on hot coals. A bannock is a Scotch bread muffin. No so-called Bannock ever called his mother's grass seed and pine nut *piki* a bannock, but a lot of the early white fur trappers were Scots, so . . ."

Longarm laughed. "So much for some sinister Bannock conspiracy out to feed us Saltu to old Piamuhmpitz."

She laughed louder, but managed not to disturb the red and black puzzle she was putting together as she said, "You *have* spent an evening or more among Ho if they've been telling you their ghost stories. But we're Tai Bha Bhon, not Saltu, to the Ho we think of as Shoshoni."

He said, "Do tell? That's odd. I thought it was the Comanche as called us Tai Bha Bhon, or Taibo."

To which she replied with a sigh, "Same difference. I told you we split them and lump them with little rhyme or reason. The name Comanche derives from something like People Who Always Want to Fight. So we applied it to plains bands calling themselves Yamparika, Kutsueka, Nokoni, Tanima, Tenawa, and a dozen other things. The famous Chief Quanah Parker is really a Kwahadi, albeit he'd agree he liked to fight all the time."

Longarm shrugged and said, "Not any more. Old Quanah's living as white as his white mamma's relations, since he got licked enough to calm him down. I *had* heard Comanche and Shoshoni started out as one nation in the Shining Times. But I got enough on my plate up Idaho way. So let's forget *other* breeds of Ho-speakers and I thank you for saving me a likely snipe hunt. Mayhaps those dudes just want an armed escort of old Indian fighters because, as you just said, a dude from back East lumps all of 'em together and couldn't tell a Paiute from a Moduc if his life depended on it, which, come to study on that, it *could*."

She agreed dudes could be silly, and added, "There, isn't this a lovely grave-gift bowl?" as she put in place the last small shard and wiped her hands on her smock.

He said it sure was, and started moving back around her work table to let himself out. She must have been able to tell he meant it—they always could—for she asked right out where he thought he was going after making up with a girl like that.

He hadn't known he had, but it would have been awfully dumb to say so. So he said, "It's almost quitting time and I doubt they'll be expecting me back at the federal building this late. So I thought I might mosey down to Romano's for some of them Eye-talian noodles they rustle up so tasty."

Sandy blushed, stared down at the grinning horror atop the table between them, and murmured, "That was where we had supper that first night you got so fresh, you fresh thing."

He nodded soberly and declared, "We could try the Golden Dragon a tad closer to Cherry Creek if you're still proddy about Romano's. Or, should push come to shove, I could likely survive dining alone this evening."

She stared up at him the way an experienced mouser regards a new gap in the baseboard while Longarm, in turn, sincerely pictured himself swirling spaghetti and sipping red ink by candlelight all by himself. For it was way easier to

31

bluff in a poker game. No man with a hard-on had ever been able to bluff any woman who'd ever seen one, and what the hell, the evening would still be young by the time he'd finished his Eye-talian almond cakes on his own.

Alexandria Henderson could see that in his amiable but independent eyes of gun-muzzle gray. For she gaily declared, "Romano's sounds fine, now that I've forgiven you for being so silly that time. But I'll have to go home and change first. Don't tell anyone, but I confess I'm only wearing my unmentionables under this heavy smock."

He agreed the weather had been warm for a Denver autumn, and asked if she'd like him to carry her on home or meet her someplace after she'd had time to gussy up.

She dimpled coyly and allowed it might save time if he escorted her to her nearby digs and waited out front while she hosed down and dressed herself up. He'd been hoping she'd say that. He didn't get upset when she sternly added that he'd better not get ideas, just because she'd been a big silly the last time she'd invited him in for a drink. A woman who wanted it couldn't bluff a grown man worth spit either.

So they never did wind up in any fancy restaurant that evening, because the stern little gal seemed to feel a man who didn't get ideas on his own could use some inspiration.

As he helped her lock up and walked her down to her quarters on Lincoln Street, Sandy somehow steered their conversation, more than once, to the topic of screwing positions.

She called it anthropology because it seemed less sassy when you used scientific-sounding words to describe what less cultivated folk were said to do.

When Longarm allowed he hadn't noticed Indians acting all that unusual, she managed to sound detached as a saw-bones peeking at a herd of germs through a microscope as she asked if he was speaking from intimate experience. That was what gals with college degrees called squaw-fucking, intimate experience.

By this time they'd made it to her rooms over the carriage house of a once-grand brownstone mansion, now divided up into less grand furnished digs. Since the fall afternoons were now so short he thumbnailed a match-head alight for the wall lamp just inside her door as he evaded her direct question by suggesting in as scientific a tone, "I meant it only stands to reason your Quill Indian still bedding down on Mother Earth, atop no more than a few thicknesses of hide or blankets, would be sore-put to go at it just the way Queen Victoria and Prince Albert might have deemed proper."

She sounded sincerely shocked as she warned him not to speak so disrespectfully of Her Majesty. So Longarm insisted, "I ain't out to low-rate the Widow of Windsor. I'm only using a high-tone white lady who managed to give birth to nine kids before her man died young as an example of formal fornication aboard fancy furniture. It was your notion to ask, just now, how come ladies sleeping less luxuriously in tipis or even pueblos tend to spare their bones some bruises by, ah, elevating their tailbones off the ground a mite."

She somehow managed to keep her tone stern as she led him into her combined sitting room and bed chamber. "That was not the proper way to describe even an Indian woman's coccyx. But are you suggesting the notoriously bestial coition of the plains culture might be inspired by no more than a dearth of proper bedding?"

He got rid of his hat but left his gun rig on as the two of them sat down on the trick sofa she could fold out into a double bed if a man played his cards right. For all he knew she'd meant what she'd said, coming down the hill, about changing her duds to dine at Romano's that evening. It was his turn to say something. So as she somehow wound up sitting closer than he'd expected, he told her, "I never met any Indian gals with cocks myself. But I have spent a night or more bedded down in a tipi, and speaking from that experience alone, I can tell you

33

that prairie sod with a blanket or more spread atop it feels proper enough for sleeping after a hard day's ride. But, well, as soon as two or more sleepers get a mite less sleepy, I reckon the results could get rough on even a white queen's tailbone. So sooner or later she'd likely ask her Prince Albert whether he'd mind too much if they finished up in a less dignified position, see?"

She didn't seem to understand, as it seemed to be getting a mite dark in there to read one another's faces. He unbuckled his gun rig to make himself more to home as he quietly explained how tough it was for a less educated cuss to delve deeper into primitive customs without sounding primitive. When he said he'd be able to show her better if only they had some Indian bedding on hand, she sprang up so suddenly he was sure he'd just shot it with that passionate but proddy little gal.

Then Sandy opened a chest in a far corner to haul out two Hudson Bay blankets and a buffalo robe, asking him how an Arapaho or Shoshoni hostess might arrange them in a tipi.

He got rid of his coat and tie as well as his gun rig on his way to join her on the floor. Kneeling at her side, Longarm showed her how to fashion a fair sleeping pallet, although he put the furry buffalo robe on top, the way white gals seemed to prefer, before he gently rolled her on her back in that denim smock to assure her in a scientific tone he was only aiming to show her what it felt like, to your average Indian lady, in the position most approved of by your average missionary.

She naturally felt obligated to protest she'd never meant to research the mores of the plains culture quite so far. But just as he'd already been told, she wasn't wearing anything but a thin sateen shimmy under that denim smock, and while she'd naturally encased her lower limbs in high-button shoes and barber-pole cotton hose, she'd felt no call to don pantaloons for her stuffy sit-down chores up to the museum. So even as she was telling him she didn't

34

want to go all the way this time, he had it in so far she sighed and demanded he at least take down those scratchy old pants, and for a short swell spell it felt just fine on the floor with him on top and both of them half dressed. But as soon as she'd come and, like the last time, felt way more at ease and hence way more like busting loose, she suggested he get off long enough for them to get more comfortable.

So he did, and she was out of her duds, save for her high-buttons and striped socks, before he could shuck his boots, the way a poor old boy had to if he meant to take off his pants entirely. So while she was waiting for more, hot as a pistol and naked as a jay, she allowed that her coccyx, as she called her tailbone, had been hammered on the floor about as often as she liked, and then, without Longarm having to tell her how, she rolled over on her hands and knees to arch her back and shyly ask if this was the way an Arapaho hostess might receive a guest.

He assured her she looked even more tempting in that position, and meant it, as he got on his knees behind her to place a tanned hand firmly on either creamy hip. For in this romantic gloom of an autumn gloaming her sweet, shapely behind was clearly visible as a sort of disembodied ass, smiling up at him through the gathering dusk, and as he penetrated her that way with renewed inspiration Sandy gasped and declared, "Heavens! It didn't feel quite as long the other way, and I have to admit that whether this is bestial or not it certainly feels heavenly!"

So it took far less persuasion, after he'd had her dog-style, to get her to playing stoop tag, squatting over him with a high-heeled high-button planted on the buffalo robe to either side of his bare hips. She said she'd make them both some scrambled eggs in time but that in the meantime, she'd kill him if he dared to go soft on her right now! So he didn't.

Patrolman Colgan O'Hanlon of the Denver Police had just noticed something out of place as he was walking his beat on the less fashionable side of Cherry Creek just after sundown.

A shadowy figure under a tall Texas hat wasn't half as concealed in the inky shade of a cottonwood across from a clean but inexpensive rooming house as he might have thought he was.

So the middle-aged copper badge, who'd survived the Great Hunger and that Great War between the Blue and Gray by moving as fast as need be, but no faster, never broke stride as he spotted whoever was up in that puddle of blackness between him and the next faint street lamp. He just kept twirling his nightstick as if without a care in the world as he swung round the next corner without a second glance at the sinister silhouette he'd have otherwise had to pass right by. For O'Hanlon knew his beat like the palm of his hand, and the yard dog chained in the back of a house on the other side of the block knew O'Hanlon well enough not to bark as the big bluff copper badge eased over its picket fence, softly calling to it, "Keep your gob shut, like the good doggy you are, and one day I might bring you a fresh bone from the Dutchman's shop across the creek."

The yard dog wagged its tail, whether it understood the soothing words or not. So O'Hanlon bent over to scratch it behind the ears before moving on, drawing the blue-steel double-action .36 he'd been issued.

Hence the next thing the somewhat taller man under the cottonwood knew O'Hanlon had the drop on him, and said so casually as he added, from his own side of yet another picket fence, "Anyone can see from your darling hat that you'd not be a Colorado rider, and so now I'd like to hear what you're doing so far from Texas and on my beat, if you take my meaning, good sir."

The stranger didn't sound at all evasive, or even surprised, as he replied without turning his head or moving either hand, "*Nochd go bragh. Agus* I'd be from County Kerry, please God."

To which O'Hanlon could only reply, "I'd be from Monaghan and that's not what I just asked you if the truth be known. Anyone but a Kerry man would know that when a copper badge asks you nicely what you'd be after doing on his beat, he wants you to tell him what you'd be after doing on his darling *beat*!"

The stranger with the Texas hat and Kerry brogue said, "In that case I'd be waiting here for another peace officer who'd be living across the street in that grand rooming house."

O'Hanlon frowned thoughtfully and said, "The only peace officer who dwells anywhere in this neighborhood would be Deputy U.S. Marshal Custis Long, the one they'd be after calling Longarm."

The stranger agreed that was who he'd been waiting for. O'Hanlon waited to hear why and, when he didn't, asked.

The stranger turned in a confiding way, allowing O'Hanlon to see more of a shadowy lantern-jawed face as he explained, "I'd be with the Texas Rangers and all and all. So I'm asking you to take the word of a fellow peace officer that the matter is a secret I'd not be at liberty to divulge."

It didn't work. The humble copper badge shrugged and replied he might believe that once he'd seen some sort of identification.

The mysterious stranger on the far side of the fence raised one hand to open his own frock coat, exposing a dim silvery blur pinned to his dark shirtfront as he chuckled fondly and said he hoped a Monaghan man recognized a Ranger badge when he saw it.

O'Hanlon made the mistake of peering closer, even as he said a real ranger would have some other identification to go with a tin star anyone might find in a pawnshop.

He knew just how right he'd been in the few instants of awareness left to him between the moment a .45–55 erupted like a volcano in his chest and when his world, and life,

37

whirled down and down in a pinwheeling kaleidoscope of ever-darker chaos.

The killer with the Texas hat and Irish brogue was already out of sight before the first windows along the street had popped open and O'Hanlon's body on the grassy side of the pickets had stopped twitching. The man who'd just killed one lawman had been about to give up on Longarm in any case. For they'd told him that unless the target of their annoyance wasn't home by moonrise, it would likely mean he'd gotten lucky at love or some other game of chance in some other part of town.

Longarm didn't seem to worry at all about healthy habits.

It made him awfully hard to kill.

shove into both his Winchester saddle gun and Colt double-action six-shooter. The .44–40 lobbed two hundred grains of lead with its forty grains of powder, hard enough to stop anything lighter on its feet than, say, a pissed-off grizzly. Many wayfaring riders favored the even lighter and hence cheaper .45–30 rounds for their good-enough Colt single-action Peacemakers. So a rascal gunning copper badges with a .45–55 read more like a hired gun than a burglar to a lawman who'd chased both in his time.

But they didn't pay Longarm to deal with local killings. So he left the killing of O'Hanlon to the Denver P.D. as he toted his saddle and other possibles over to the Burlington yards late in the afternoon. They allowed him six cents a mile traveling alone. So he came out ahead if he traveled free, and that was easier to work out when a good old boy bought a beer now and again for a certain freight dispatcher he usually found a good quarter mile catty-corner from the regular ticket office off the waiting room of the Union Depot.

That was why Longarm left for Cheyenne aboard the caboose of a way freight almost an hour before the passenger train a greenhorn might have to pay his way aboard pulled out. And that was why a hard-eyed gent wearing a new hat but the same .45–55 failed to spot Longarm anywhere amid the folks boarding almost an hour after Longarm had left town.

Way freights, as their name indicated, took their own sweet time as they poked up the line, stopping along the way. So Longarm's free ride was on a siding near Fort Collins, dropping off some bob-wire and ladies' notions, when the passenger train overtook them and roared grandly by. But Longarm didn't care. He'd planned on an overnight stay in Cheyenne with a certain brunette who dwelt alone, and it was smarter to show up with a sack of gumdrops and mayhaps some flowers *after* supper time.

He felt he was still likely to beat those Eastern dudes to the rail junction at Ogden, west of the Divide, if the

41

brunette asked him to stay over for the whole weekend. If he was wrong and the party started north into Indian country without him, he'd doubtless catch up with them in a day or so along the trail, knowing a shortcut or more after scouting in the recent Shoshoni Scare.

So once again, without knowing he was doing it, Longarm escaped a swell ambush they'd set up for him in Ogden.

Trisha, the gal he knew in Cheyenne, would have deserved some of the credit, had either of them known what else she was doing for an old pal as she served him home-cooked meals and other delights in bed for a good three nights and two whole days. When he finally boarded his ride to Ogden, walking a mite funny after all that riding, Longarm had no call to suspect someone might be laying for him up ahead. His reasons for dropping off at Huntsville, a few miles east of Ogden, were less devious. After a good tedious rest aboard yet another way freight he was feeling restless, and so, needing to hire some horseflesh in any case, he toted his McClellan and such over to a livery corral within sight of the tracks to see what sort of deal he might make this far from the bright lights of Ogden, with a population as high as two thousand when the herds were in town.

The Mormons who mostly hired horseflesh to other saintly members of their sect didn't cotton to the notion of hiring Longarm any at any price until they tumbled to just who he was. Once they had, they allowed that a dollar a week a head, with no deposit, sounded about right for a gentile lawman in good with the elders of their main temple in Salt Lake. Longarm had dealt firmly but fairly with a wayward Saint or gentile outlaw out this way in the past and, to the relief of many a Mormon, he'd done so without either low-rating their somewhat unusual faith or pretending to believe every word of it. When he allowed that he'd neither smoke inside their city limits nor throw every three-for-a-nickel cheroot away, they allowed that sounded fair, as long as he didn't teach their livestock to chew tobacco or sip tea on the sly.

When he told them where he was headed they agreed he'd make the best time riding one horse and leading a lighter-packed spare. When they suggested a pair of fourteen-hand geldings, one a paint and one a roan, both with obvious cayuse bloodlines, Longarm almost said he could see they knew which end of a pony the shit fell out of. But he never did, because Mormons didn't hold with rough talk either.

He road down Twelve Mile Creek into Ogden aboard the paint and leading the roan, with no trail supplies as yet. He knew that just as it was smarter to hire livestock a ways out of town, it could be dumb to buy trail fodder and canned goods at a country store that paid extra wagon-freight charges from the nearest railroad.

He knew that whether he'd beaten those others to Ogden or vice versa, it made more sense to ask at the Land Office, where he'd been told they'd all wind up. So he naturally rode into town well clear of the railroad depot, and hence had no idea anyone could be waiting for him there with an innocent expression and a brace of Merwin Hulbert horse pistols.

When he strode into the Land Office a snippy young priss pushing pencils for the Bureau of Land Management demanded to know where in thunder he'd been all this time, as if it was any of his business, and said the dudes he'd been detailed to ride with had ridden out the day before, tired of waiting for him and mighty vexed with him as well.

So Longarm left without wasting more time in useless excuses, and stopped at the first general store he came upon to stock up on trail supplies at outrageous cost, lest anyone get more outraged at him. Then he swapped pack and riding saddles and lit out for Fort Hall the rougher but shorter way he recalled of old. So that was how come yet another dry-gulcher, lying in wait for him atop an outcrop overlooking the stage route out of Ogden with a scope-sighted Big Fifty buffalo rifle, got to wait, and wait, and then wait some more. Meanwhile, Longarm rode up the far side of the Bear River, through willows and worse, in a serious effort

43

to overtake the government party some-damned-where this side of total disaster.

He wasn't expecting any Indian trouble this side of Fort Hall. He knew it would be a total disaster for him if they got as far as Fort Hall without him, and Billy Vail ever found out they had.

Chapter 5

The only stretch of the Bear River Longarm cared about at the moment ran north to south into the Great Salt Lake. He'd forded to the less-settled west side of the Bear before heading upstream, though the stage and freight route north ran east of the river. For the stage and freight route snaked and stopped at countless crossings as it served the northern end of the aptly named Mormon Delta.

The Mormon Delta was more a long green ribbon running north and south along the aprons of the mountains to the east than a D-shaped patch of irrigated crop and pasture land. Starting a day or so after they'd found their Utopia in the sagebrush wasteland between the Rockies and the distant Sierra Nevadas, the Mormons had commenced to dam and ditch like gophers full of locoweed, until one day there wasn't a wasteland anymore between the foothills and a western border formed by the Bear, the Great Salt Lake, and the drier Sevier, Beaver, and such to the south. Hundred of irrigation ditches, wide and narrow, cut the Mormon Delta into a patchwork of firm to soggy fields it wasn't considered neighborly to cut across. But since a rider found few if any such obstacles on the open sage flats west of the river, Longarm could beeline, making far better time, hitting a bend of the Bear no more often than his ponies needed a water break—and that wasn't all that often, given stock with cayuse blood in sunny but not too sunny riding weather.

He rode all day, swapping mounts every eight or ten miles, and felt tempted to cut back across the Bear by sundown, figuring he should have overtaken the others, despite their lead, by this time. But then he considered they wouldn't *have* any confounded lead if he hadn't been overconfident up until then. So he forged on through the gathering dusk, through stirrup-deep sage, till his ponies needed a rest whether he did or not.

He made a cold camp in the middle of a sage flat because of the infernal cheat grass.

The ponies didn't care, once he'd watered them from carefully hoarded water bags and filled their nose bags with the real oats he'd bought them back in Ogden. He tethered them to deep-rooted sage clumps and spread his bedding atop cheat, upwind to the east. The night was crisp but not really bitter, and canned beans washed down with tomato preserves didn't require a fire either. He didn't need black coffee to put himself to sleep, and it wasn't a good idea to smoke in these parts either. It wasn't just that the Book of Mormon frowned on smoking and drinking anything stronger than, say, buttermilk. The former theocracy of Deseret, now Utah Territory, had been turned into a tinderbox by the unwelcome advance of an Old World annual after it had found its true vocation as another pernicious weed of the American West.

It was called chess—or cheat grass, because that was what it did. It hogged such scarce rain as the Great Basin got, to explode from the ash-gray soil as lush and green as Kentucky blue after a nice wet spring. But there was more thin sap than substance to cheat, even when it was green, and in no time at all it set too few seeds to matter and died back to tasteless straw that was mostly air and caught on fire every chance it got.

It wouldn't even stay springy under the bones of a weary traveler. So Longarm woke up stiff as well as early. After

46

that he watered the ponies again, broke camp, and rode on, sucking his own breakfast from the cans, atop the roan.

He was tempted to swing over into the delta and see if anyone else had made it this far north out of Ogden yet. But for all he knew the Easterners were cavalry vets on Tennessee walkers. So Longarm forged on, and on, all day, until he felt sure he'd crossed the Idaho line, and swung east around sundown to chase his own and other purple shadows across the swift but shallow Bear in hopes of beating those other birds into Zion.

He did. Zion was a small but thriving Mormon settlement a tad off the map of Utah Territory. Mormons were like that. They had this calling to make the desert blossom as the rose, and put whole towns in the last places any other white folks might pick. So he'd even met up with Mormons south of the border, raising a bodacious crop of kids and corn in the Sonora Desert.

The ones around Zion seemed more interested in wheat, unless that was barley stubble in the harvested fields he saw all around as he rode in by moonrise. The country was too high for profitable corn crops. Gentile homesteaders might have held it was too bumpy for any field crops at all. But coming from West-by-God-Virginia, Longarm knew a family could scratch a bushel here and another yonder, as long as they used hand tools instead of a plow where they had a time standing upright without hanging on to something.

Since coming West after the war, Longarm had decided it made a heap more sense grazing stock in country this high and dry. But of course the Latter-day Saints would recruit new converts from such outlandish parts as the British Isles, and most of their elders had started out as Eastern farm boys to begin with.

He saw some beef grazing closer to town as he rode toward the soft, shimmering lamplights ahead. The contented-looking beef were shorter of horn and whiter of face than one saw grazing out on open range in these parts.

But the stockmen around Zion seemed to raise beef on their own irrigated grass, inside bob-wire, so it was likely safe for a short-horned steer to gorge itself so fat if it wasn't likely to stand off any range wolves on its own.

There were still folks up and about as Longarm rode into what they were starting to call the seat of Zion County in the Territory of Idaho, a recent part of the once-enormous Oregon. Longarm knew better than to ask directions to the nearest saloon in a Mormon settlement. But when he asked a kid in bib overalls for directions to the best place to meet other strangers in town, the kid told him to try the stage stop, where they stayed open to all hours and even served coffee, as long as it was only to outsiders just passing through.

Longarm thanked the Mormon kid and rode on without wasting time on livery matters. He knew any place that catered to the stagecoach trade would surely be willing and able to water, fodder, and stall a couple of extra ponies.

He found his way by the lantern lights from the windows of the private homes all about. There wasn't much of a business district for the number of families that lived bee-swarmed together the way farm folks dwelt back in the old countries across the big water. It made a lot of sense in Indian country. White outlaws were even more likely to hit isolated spreads, now that the Indian wars had commenced to wind down. The Mormon folks behind those lamplit lace curtains all around were doubtless more secure and likely felt a lot less edgy late at night with the winds making funny noises in the hills all around.

Somewhere someone had baked an apple pie, and like many another traveling man, Longarm had always felt most wistful about his own lone riding when riding by a lamplit window just around bedtime while sort of wondering who might be going to bed with whom inside.

It didn't really help to tell himself he'd never be really happy settled down in Mormon long underwear with any gal who wore the same to bed and wouldn't even let him smoke afterwards. It didn't help, if it was true or not, to consider that most gals willing to serve a man coffee and climb into bed with him bare-ass were sort of plain to begin with, and inclined to nag after the first few weeks no matter what they looked like. He was starting to feel horny again, and a stranger could get in trouble with the kith and kin of any small-town gal of any persuasion.

He cheered up a mite when he spied the more imposing sprawl of the layover stop Overland had built in such an out-of-the-way spot. The Overland Line had fallen on hard times since they'd had to compete with the Iron Horse. But in its day they'd had the only means to move mail, freight, or passengers between Salt Lake City and the Montana gold fields. So they'd been well able to build adequately, and since they still carried plenty of light freight and impatient mining men across what was still a shortcut, they made enough to maintain the layout there in Zion.

But Overland didn't do so much business these days that they'd be too proud to overnight a pair of strange ponies. After Longarm had negotiated that, he discovered they'd be willing to water, fodder, and overnight *him* at a modest price as well. A layover built when the Overland stages had run every day, both ways, was in no position to turn travelers away from its door now that the Concords only came through half empty no more than thrice a week.

Harking back to the heyday of stagecoach travel, this installation, where they'd not only paused to change teams, but had gotten off to enjoy a late supper and an early breakfast with a few hours' sleep between, was as much a wayside inn as a repair shop, smithy, and livery stable, with a stock farm out back. But Longarm was still pleasantly surprised, once he'd checked in and stowed his valuables upstairs. He found they ran their downstairs dining room more in the style of the Montana gold fields to the northeast than the Mormons all about might approve. The willowy ash-blonde who presided over the dining room in a chocolate-brown dress and fresh white apron told him they served far more Montana mining men than Mormon farmers in there of an evening. He believed her when she not only said he could have all the black coffee he wanted with his sit-down supper, but asked if he liked his coffee laced with bourbon in the high-toned Irish manner.

He said he did. He didn't want her to think him a sissy, and in any case he'd be a bit too keyed up to go to bed alone after sipping black coffee with nothing in it to steady the nerves.

After they got that settled he ordered their special of mule-deer chops and a canned vegetable of his choice as long as it was green peas or wax beans. He told her to forget the rabbit fodder, and asked whether they got their fresher grub from the locals.

She said, "Local Indians. Boss has a deal with some of that old Pocatello's Snakes. You'd be surprised how many sides of venison those Indians will swap for just a keg of firewater."

Longarm almost said he wouldn't. But it was none of his beeswax unless and until the B.I.A. or Revenue Service said so.

He didn't ask what Shoshoni might be doing this far south of their official reservation either. She'd just now told him the Indians seemed to be trading. He waited until the sort of plain gal had come back with his supper before he asked about those other whites he'd hoped to catch up with here.

She wasn't all that plain when she smiled, sort of wistfully, and assured him she'd have remembered any party of six or eight Easterners, or even Westerners, passing through. One got the impression business had been slow at that Overland stop of late. He said they'd told him much the same at the desk out front, but that sometimes riders in a hurry just paused for a bite before riding on, without bedding down in town at all. She said lots of saddle tramps passing through did that a lot, and asked him who all his pals in such a hurry might be.

50

He washed down some mule deer with black coffee and explained they weren't exactly pals of his. He said, "I've never laid eyes on any of 'em, far as I know. If I ever do, we're all of us headed up to Fort Hall for some sort of powwow with the same old boys you get your groceries from."

For some reason that seemed to fluster her. She spent a long time in the kitchen just to fetch a man's serviceberry pie with mousetrap cheese.

But once she did get back, with a mighty generous helping of dessert, she was smiling fit to bust and admiring the blazes out of him with her big blue eyes while she asked, in a mighty worried tone, if he might be a lawman.

He chuckled fondly and replied, "I'd be Deputy U.S. Marshal Custis Long out of the Denver office, ma'am. I'm sorry I never said so sooner. But to answer what they really wanted you to ask me out in the kitchen, I don't worry all that much about a friendly trading off his agency, with or without the full a approval of his agent. Friendly or hostile are the words I'm interested in, on account I've tangled with hostile Shoshoni in my time and all in all I prefer the other kind."

She gulped and said she'd only spoken in jest about firewater. So he assured her he'd assumed as much, and insisted on her naming a price for all that swell grub no matter what her boss out in the kitchen said about feeling patriotic.

So they settled on seventy-five cents, tip included, and he went out front to sit on the steps a spell, wishing he could smoke and wondering where in thunder those others might be.

When a distant bell tolled ten times Longarm knew that whereever they were, they'd have dismounted for the night by this time. So he got back up, went back inside, and ambled back for more Irish coffee with a smoke, only to find the lamps all trimmed with the chairs stacked upside down on all the tables. So he went on up to his hired room, early as it still might be.

The willowy ash-blonde from downstairs was waiting for him, already in bed with her long, lank hair unpinned and down around her bare shoulders. She hadn't worn that dining-room outfit or anything else to bed, as far as he could tell from his own side of the cotton sheet and maroon flannel blanket she was holding over her tits. She looked sort of coy as she demurely said, "Whatever kept you down there all this time? It feels as if I've been waiting up here for hours!"

To which Longarm could only reply, "You have. They really must be worried about us pestering them about a little trade liquor if they ordered you up here to compromise me. That's what they call it when a lawman can't testify against folks because he's fucked 'em. Compromising."

She covered her face with her hands and began to bawl. He took off his hat and coat but left his six-gun right where it was as he bolted the door and sat down on the bed beside her, gently telling her, "There was no delicate way to put it, and you must have known what they meant you to do with me when they told you to take off your duds, climb into my bed, and await my pleasure."

She sobbed, "I'm not what you think I am! I'm not! I'm not! I got myself into this dreadful fix by giving away family secrets to a stranger before I knew who he was!"

Longarm placed a soothing palm on one of her shaking naked shoulders, "Don't be so rough on yourself. I know you ain't a real whore, no offense. Gals in the habit of spreading their warm thighs for cold cash lack the ambition to wait tables for honest wages. And as for you blabbing a mite because you have so few chances to talk to anyone down yonder, I'd have found out in any case. Indians full of firewater gossip way worse than any white woman I've ever gossiped with. But like I said before, I got no call to pester Indians that ain't doing anything I'd arrest your average white man for doing."

"Then we're still friends?" she pleaded, letting one nipple pop out into the lamplight in a mighty friendly way as she put a hand to the hand he'd placed on her shoulder to slide it down the front of her all the way.

He'd been right about her not having anything on under those covers. He sighed and balled the hand she was tempting into as firm a fist as he could manage, knowing she'd never get it in down yonder now. Then he quietly but firmly told her, "Friendly is just as friendly as friendly acts, ma'am. I told you I didn't want to be compromised too, remember?"

She began to rub her moist love-slit up and down the knuckles of his manly fist as she pleaded, "Call me Zelda, and now that you've been so nice I don't feel half as awkward about all this, ah, Custis?"

He smiled thinly and replied, "Speak for yourself, Miss Zelda. I got a boner for you that feels awkward as anything. So why don't I just step outside long enough for you to get up, get dressed, and get out of here before we both wind up in an awkward position!"

She started to rub herself with his knuckles harder as she shut her eyes and groaned between gritted teeth, "It wouldn't seem so awkward now that I've gotten used to the idea. What's the matter with you? Don't you want to?"

He soberly replied, "I'd be lying if I said I'd rather stick it in a pail of water, Miss Zelda. But I'll be compromised if I even jack you off all the way, so let go my hand, let me duck outside the way I said, and we'll just say no more about it."

She sobbed, "It's too late! I'm coming!" So he snatched his wet fist from her gushing snatch and sprang to his feet to unlatch the door and slip out into the dark hallway.

He didn't know the big fat cuss standing there in an apron with a shit-eating smile, but he figured who it had to be and told the kitchen boss, "It's a good thing for you I know better than to hit an asshole I might have to testify against in the future. So pay attention, asshole.

I just told your wife, daughter, or whatever I didn't ride for Indian Affairs or Revenue, but I'd be proud to turn such a low-down pimp in for running firewater to wards of the government if I didn't have so many Indian pals and such a live-and-let-live nature."

The fat oaf who'd sent the much younger blonde up to screw him then said, "I don't know what you're fussing at me for, stranger. That sassy Zelda will say most anything to get next to a man. But she was lying if she said anything about serving strong drink to Indians downstairs. We don't serve Indians at all, and even if we did, ain't it against federal law to serve 'em anything strong as beer?"

Longarm snorted in disgust and replied, "We've agreed it's sort of silly. Now quit acting silly with me and listen tight. I'll be sending your Zelda back down to you as pure as ever I found her, if ever I can get her out of my damned bed. You'll note I haven't had the pleasure of slapping you sensible neither. And so, in sum, it didn't work, I'm still free to accuse you in open court of running doubtless-untaxed corn squeezings to Lord knows who all in a Mormon-run county, and I mean to if I have any more trouble from you all!"

The worried-looking fat man protested, "Jesus H. Christ, after we offered to feed you for nothing and sent a great lay up to your room, you say we've been trying to give you *trouble*?"

Longarm answered, with a weary sigh, "I did and you have. I don't want to repeat what I just told Miss Zelda about compromising a peace officer with swell presents and pussy. Suffice it to say, my flesh may be weak but my spirit carries a badge. So I want you to vanish forever from my sight, and meanwhile, I'll see why that other pest is taking so long."

Longarm ducked back inside without waiting to see whether his last command to the kitchen boss had been obeyed. He saw right off why Zelda was still there. She'd gotten out of bed but she hadn't put anything on and she was an ash-blonde all over as she stood there bold as brass and barefoot, defying him to say he didn't want her now.

To which Longarm could only reply, with a weary smile, "I never said I was a celibate monk, Miss Zelda. I said I was a lawman, on duty, who couldn't fuck with a known lawbreaker whether he wanted to or not."

She purred something about it hardly mattering since he'd said he felt no call to turn her in. So he found her duds atop her low-cut work shoes in one corner, and scooped them up in one bundle so he could grab her bare elbow with his other hand and steer her for the doorway while she protested he couldn't shove a naked lady out in the hallway as if she was some sort of trash.

But he could. So he did saying, "Aw, you ain't no lady, even if you are buck-naked, and the trash who sent you to buy off the law with some slap and tickle would know better than me what sort of trash you are."

Then he let go of her, her duds, and her shoes to crawfish back inside and slam the door with a grin as her wild swipe with clawed nails whipped through the empty space he'd just had his face in.

His grin faded as he bolted the door on the inside again while she bawled dreadful things about his manhood on the other side.

He was too proud, or perhaps too ashamed, to yell back he still had an erection Casanova might have been anxious to display as his own at one of his fancy French gatherings. He'd done what a man just had to do, at least with some women, and it was nobody's beeswax how damned stiff his old organ-grinder might be, or what he might be going to do about that now.

Chapter 6

A possibly sane old hermit who'd read the Good Book every night had once assured a much younger Custis Long that the Lord had not slain Onan, son of Judah, just for jacking off that time. The true sin of Onan, as soon as one studied on it, was the way a spiteful son of a bitch had jacked off smack in front of the poor widow woman the Lord had just commanded him to come in.

It stood to reason that a Lord who took plain and simple jacking off hard would have wiped out the whole human race before poor Onan was ever born, for as some prophet had once written, "Nine out of ten people play with themselves and that tenth one is a liar."

But Longarm managed not to that night, because of other considerations. It was true you didn't have to look your best or promise your hand you'd respect it in the morning, but as another prophet had written, likely in French, "Never jack off in the morning. You never know who you might meet at lunch."

A much younger Longarm had once been sore as hell at himself at a hotel fire, after meeting up after midnight with another guest who'd likely strummed herself to sleep just down the hall, unaware of how surprising life can get. So that night in Zion Longarm just sat on his damned windowsill, smoking in the dark and considering all the trouble he might have just avoided, till he fell into bed too weary to care and hence woke up the next morning with an even stiffer one.

He just felt silly about that till he went downstairs to see if they'd still serve him some breakfast.

They wouldn't. The chairs were still stacked on the tables in the dining room, and when he stuck his head in the kitchen to ask how come, there was nobody there. He could tell by the cold clammy smell that they'd let the cast-iron range burn itself out entirely and they'd padlocked the far door to the pantry and root cellar.

It was true few if any wayfarers would show up for breakfast at an overnight stop they never stopped at. But Longarm had seen other names in the guest book when he'd signed in the night before, and even if he had been the only overnight guest, it seemed a tad unusual to let a wood-fed kitchen range cool down all the way if they ever meant to cook anything later in the day. For those heavy-duty ranges meant for serious restaurant cooking took their own sweet time to warm up, once you let them cool down to the temperature of Idaho in autumn.

He drifted out to the front desk, lighting a cheroot in hopes of staving off starvation till he could find somewhere else or, failing that, open a can of pork and beans up in his room. The big lobby, which doubled as a waiting room for the stage line, was a tad less clammy, thanks to a thoughtful fire of snapping and hissing pine logs in the big potbellied stove they'd planted smack in the middle of the cavernous space. Four earlier risers were seated around the potbelly. The only one worth looking at twice looked at least as hungry and twice as sore as Longarm. After that she was a high-toned beauty in a sidesaddle riding habit of loden green that made her auburn hair look more so. She wore that upswept, under a perky black derby held in such a precarious position by the veil that covered her cameo features as far down as her perky nose. As he stood there admiring her from the doorway with his morning hard-on, she favored him with a frosty smile and asked if he worked for Overland. Her accent was hoity-toity British, and her tone was so cold he was glad he could deny the charge.

Once he had, he said, "I'm in the market for a good breakfast as well, ma'am. There ain't nobody in the kitchen, this morning. I ain't tried to find the manager yet. So why don't you all sit tight and I'll let you know as soon as I find out what's happened."

Neither the gal in green nor her drabber fellow travelers put up any argument. So Longarm ambled over to the desk by the front entrance, banged on the bell a few times, and when that failed to get results, strode through a far archway, yelling for some damned service. At that the room clerk from the night before stuck a bald head out his door to protest, "What's all this racket? Ain't Zelda minding the damned front as well as the dining room? It ain't as if this place gets all that busy this side of the evening stage, you know."

Noting the poor confused cuss was still wearing his nightshirt in the chill morning air, Longarm explained, "Ain't nobody here but five hungry guests, including me. Am I safe in assuming your missing mess staff might not be on the Overland payroll as regular help?"

The clerk nodded. "You are. I'm the manager here, and I make all the arrangements. Overland is interested in moving mail, freight, and passengers in that order. *Feeding* the sons of bitches has never been too profitable. So the company would as soon let others worry about that, on concession contracts. What might that have to do with the Robbins family running out on us so unexpected?"

Longarm asked more about the missing bunch, and established they were talking about Zelda, a half-wit they said was her brother, and an aunt and uncle named Robbins. Then he said, "It must have been guilty conscience, compounded by my unexpected willpower most likely. Miss Zelda's brother ain't the only dumb one in the family. But now that I think back, I ain't sure what she told me was the only federal offense they were worried about. I wonder what I'd have found out if I'd spent a tad more time with that dishwater blonde they tried to tempt me with."

Then he took another drag on his almost-spent cheroot, shrugged, and added, "Be that as it may, they've lit out somewhere and it's past my usual breakfast time. So might there be another restaurant open at this hour in your fair city?"

The Overland man, being another gentile, felt free to laugh and make sneering reference to the odds on that in a close-knit little Mormon settlement. "Up to just a few minutes ago I'd have said this was the only place in Zion you could ask for coffee with your ham and eggs, or smoke afterwards. The local Mormons have their own places to eat all the meals a Mormon would want. They eat at home. Gentiles passing through have always eaten here. So I'll be switched if I can tell you where me and my Lulu are going to have breakfast once we get up."

Longarm asked about the stable help. He wasn't surprised to learn all but one of them were Mormons who doubtless ate at home whenever the spirit moved them. He sent the manager back to bed with his Lulu and went up to his own room to gather some makings before he went back down to the main room, where the original four others had been joined by a confounded-looking breed kid in overalls. Longarm asked the kid if he was a stable hand. When the kid allowed he was and asked where Uncle Pete Robbins had run off to, Longarm smiled and decided, "You'd know better than me whether they left serious by wagon or light on ponies, old son."

The kid said he hadn't seen them leaving. A Mormon hand had been the first to notice, just a few minutes ago, when he'd stopped by the kitchen on his own way to work that morning. The breed kid said the Robbins family lived on the outskirts of town, and that he just didn't know that much about any riding or rolling stock they might have had handy at home.

So Longarm took a battered coffeepot out of the feed sack he'd brought down from his room and handed it to the young breed, saying, "If you'd like to fill this pot from the pump out back, I got some Arbuckle Brand coffee here for one and all."

Even the snooty-looking British gal brightened up as Longarm dug deeper, producing the canned goods he'd brought down as well. When she asked how much he wanted for a "tin," as she put it, Longarm told her, "Nobody gets a whole can of nothing, if we mean to make ends meet, ma'am. I got some tin plates in here somewhere, and if we share out these pork and beans, bully beef, sardines, and tomato preserves . . . What are you waiting on, boy? Don't you want no infernal coffee with your breakfast?"

The kid lit out with the pot as if he'd been stuck with a pin. The auburn-headed beauty laughed knowingly and said, "One can see you must have been an officer in your recent Civil War. My father served in the Sepoy Mutiny with the Queen's Own 79th, and do you really eat sardines mixed with corned beef for breakfast in America?"

He hunkered down to get to work with the can-opener blade of his pocket knife as he replied in as amused a tone, "Only when we can't shoot a muskrat or a yummy wolverine for breakfast, ma'am. On occasions such as this you eat what you can get, unless you'd as soon just listen to your innards growl till you can find some filet mignon with an amusing wine."

She sucked in her breath and her green eyes blazed a mite as he continued dryly. "As for your other questions, that war don't seem so recent to those of us who run off to it, young and foolish. I disremember which side I rode with, but I'm sure I was never no officer. I reckon I got used to giving orders later. I've been a trail boss in my time, and for the last six or eight years I've had to order others about as a federal lawman. I'd be Deputy U.S. Marshal Custis Long, ma'am."

She said in that case she'd be Dame Flora MacSorley of some glen and some lady-protecting society of some town in Scotland. Then she introduced a homely little sparrow gal sitting farther from the potbelly as her personal maid, and said the middle-aged gent with the muttonchop whiskers and slate-blue Tam o' Shanter hat was named Angus and was a retainer. The old coot ignored Longarm's offer to shake and said something in either Erse or English.

The other middle-aged gent, dressed more sensibly for riding in the high country, was the guide Dame Flora had hired down by Salt Lake. He was a gentile of the Hebrew persuasion called Rhinegold. When Longarm asked if he was any kin to Johnny Ringo, he chuckled and said he'd heard that other Rhinegold might be Jewish but that they'd never met and that he hoped they never would.

The kid came back with the coffeepot. Longarm told him to put it atop the infernal stove if he expected the water to boil. By the time he'd doled out a mixed dish of canned grub tasting just as good, or bad, cold, he had a better notion why Dame Flora hadn't wanted a Mormon guide leading her expedition up to this end of the Mormon Delta.

Glad to learn Longarm was a federal lawman owing no allegiance to the Church of Jesus Christ of Latter-day Saints, as the Mormans called themselves officially, the auburn-haired lady from Scotland confided she was on a mission for her society. Back in Scotland they suspected Mormon harem masters were keeping young Scotch gals as white slaves after luring them out to the Great American Desert with all sorts of big fibs.

Longarm handed out the last tin plate and rose to drop a fistful of ground coffee in the pot atop the stove as he said, "I buy Arbuckle Brand because it's meant for brewing crude along the trail, ma'am. As for Mormons keeping harems of captive white or even red gals out this way, I thought your own famous explorer, Richard Burton of British Intelligence, looked into that for Her Majesty a spell back, whilst Brother Brigham was still alive and living in dubious bliss with those twenty-seven ladies who'd married up with him, willing."

Dame Flora sniffed in a high-toned way and said, "Black Dick Burton is hardly the one I'd trust to investigate dirty old men, after reading his scandalous accounts of Oriental domestic habits. And didn't that twenty-seventh wife escape from the clutches of Brigham Young?"

Longarm shook his head. "Nope. She left him plain and simple with nobody trying to stop her. Then she wrote a book that was scandalous in its own right, and went on the vaudeville stage for a few years, entertaining folks with tales of her mistreatment by a whole mess of dirty old men."

He checked the coffeepot, saw it had to simmer some more, and added, "So much for tales of Brother Brigham sending his Danites or Avenging Angels after anyone who told tales out of school. That twenty-seventh wife was on a regular vaudeville circuit, with handbills and posters distributed well ahead to let everyone know just where she'd be mean-mouthing the Mormons next. Whether they cared or not they never bothered her, and she *still* lectures on the tedious topic of a dead man's desire for her fair white body now and again. The public ain't as interested as it once was, now that a second generation of Mormons seem to be running Utah Territory with a tad less zeal."

Dame Flora didn't seem at all convinced, and by the time the coffee had been brewed and drunk she'd told a tale that had Longarm a tad worried as well.

Like other churches, the Latter-day Saints sent missionaries out to save the heathens in outlandish parts of the world. But maybe because they were starting from sort of an outlandish part themselves, the Great American Desert, Mormon missionaries did a lot of converting in the British Isles. There the heathens started out with the advantage of already knowing how to read The Book, and a bemused local government was more likely to send Captain Richard

Burton than a whole U.S. Cavalry column to investigate any problems.

Burton had figured he'd done enough with the publication of his *City of the Saints,* in which he allowed he'd found the Mormons not better nor worse than most bloody Yanks. But Dame Flora had been sent to follow up on more disturbing recent rumors about the final fates of Scotch spinster gals who'd been recruited by mail as Mormon converts and harem beauties.

When Longarm chuckled at the picture, Dame Flora sternly pointed out that she found it more pathetic than silly, since it seemed all too true most of the women involved were either too long in the tooth or simply too plain to get any Scotchman to look at them. The much better-looking Dame Flora said the new converts had been required to pay their own way over sea and land to far-off romantic Deseret, where they'd be claimed as brides by Mormon planters or ranchers too busy with their vast estates to ride into town to meet gals like everyone else did.

Longarm's eyebrows didn't go up high till Dame Flora got to the part about dowries. It seemed these mysterious Mormon moguls weren't ready to marry just any old gal, hard up as they might be. The lonesome spinsters from far-off Aberdeen and Inverness were supposed to show up with substantial dowries, at least a hundred pounds, five hundred bucks as they counted money in Deseret.

Longarm agreed that sounded substantial in a West where a dance-hall gal could usually find a plain-but honest husband if she wanted to, wasn't deformed, and took a bath at least once a week.

He explained, "The Mormons don't convert by mail order, ma'am. I've known some Mormon missionaries both sensible and pesky, so I can tell you they convert in person, on the spot. The Salt Lake Temple sends young elders out in teams, and I know they got a regular mission in London Town. You'd have to ask Salt Lake if they've built one up in Scotland by now."

She said, "We *have* asked. They informed us they've saved some souls, as they put it, in our industrial area around Glasgow. They deny any knowledge of Mormon missionaries operating in the Highlands and, like you, claim they've never heard of any Mormons sending for mail-order brides, with or without dowries."

So Longarm said, "There you go then, ma'am. Some-one's played a cruel hoax on lonesome Scotch gals. Most likely from somewhere way closer to Scotland. Sounds like a college-boy prank to me."

"Not a few envelopes with American stamps and Salt Lake City postmarks have been forwarded to my society by worried relatives of the missing girls," she said, "We're talking about at least two dozen missing girls, as of my leaving for your own country with Angus and Jeannie here. Like yourself and Black Dick Burton before us, we found the Mormon authorities friendly and cooperative, or pretending to be, when we arrived in Salt Lake City a week ago."

"They learned their lesson during the Mormon Wars," the gentile called Rhinegold chimed in. Then he winked and said, "It's like fighting smoke with a club. The main temple claims to keep files on every Mormon and all his ancestors back to Adam, but as soon as Miss Flora here got to asking about Mormons on her list, they dummied up and said they'd never heard of any of 'em!"

Dame Flora nodded firmly. Longarm suggested, "It works as well another way, ma'am. Using the U.S. mails to defraud is a federal offense, and it can't be all that legal under the laws of Utah. So might it not be logical for a rascal out to hoax a lady by mail to write her under an assumed name?"

Dame Flora shrugged. "The Mormon elders we spoke with in Salt Lake City suggested much the same thing. *Our* point is that someone out this way answered inquiries from a good many interested and not-so-young ladies, each of whom shipped out for America with at least five hundred

65

Yankee dollars, never to be seen alive again by anyone we can find."

Longarm whistled thoughtfully and calculated, "Meaning at least six thousand dollars can't be accounted for. I'm sorry to say I follow your drift. But may I ask what you all might be doing up here in Idaho Territory if those missing gals and their modest fortunes were last seen headed for Salt Lake City?"

Rhinegold said, "I can answer that. Seems one of the missing Scotch gals managed to post a letter for help. Sent from Zion County, Idaho Territory, judging from the postmark. She must not have deemed it safe to put a return address on the envelope."

Dame Flora said, "It was a short, frantic note. She wrote it would be dropped in the box at the next stagecoach stop if she got the chance."

Longarm pointed at the empty tin cups and greasy plates with a meaningful glance at the young stable hand he'd just fed for free. Then he mused aloud, "Reckon a gal could scribble a note in the dark in front of other travelers, if she put her mind to it. Could have dropped it most anywhere along the Overland route, long as it had a postage stamp on it, and she wouldn't have had to come this way by stage, as soon as you study on what all of *us* are doing here in this stage stop this morning."

Dame Flora said she'd already figured that. When she said she and her companions had been trying to find someone up this way who recalled even one other Scotch lady, traveling in any direction way with or without a Mormon husband, Longarm said he wasn't surprised they'd had no luck. "Kidnappers don't allow their victims to jaw all that much with strangers along the trail. If any of those gals had got to jaw a lot with anyone you're likely to find, you'll likely find they ain't been kidnapped. Do you mind it I smoke, Dame Flora?"

When she nodded her permission, Longarm offered cheroots to the other two grown men, the kid having left by then with the dirty dishes, and lit up to give himself some time to ponder before he went on. "Say a gal in trouble got a chance to drop a note in some mail slot this side of the Utah line but south of, say, Soda Springs. The Overland stage could have carried it out by way of Utah or Montana Territory, depending on which way the stage, not necessarily the gal, was going. That don't leave you many to question about strange white gals in a country where even a handsome Indian gal is worth noting in passing. What did her note say?"

Dame Flora said, "I don't have it with me. But it was simply a few scrawled lines, in broad Scots, to the effect that she'd been betrayed and warning a kinswoman who'd been planning a similar mistake to inform Her Majesty's Government instead."

Longarm admitted he didn't know just what she meant by Broad Scots. So she explained, "Think of it as a dialect neither speakers of the Queen's English nor Scots Gaelic can follow without pain. I suspect she used antiquated crofter terms in case her captors got ahold of her note before she could post it. So you'll have to take my word a 'moss trooper' is a rustic you'd never want your sister to marry, and a Sawny Bean is worse!"

She repressed a shudder and added, "I hope she only meant the band of outlaws who waylaid, robbed, and murdered travelers on a lonely road in Scotland in the sixteen hundreds. I'd hate to think any of those poor girls had actually been dismembered and *eaten* by a wolf pack of half-witted cannibals!"

Longarm perked up to say, "Oh, I recall reading about your Sawny Bean and his clan of cave dwellers. They remind me of the Bender family we used to have over in Kansas, albeit I doubt Kate Bender and her kin ever got around to eating any of the travelers they murdered and buried on their remote prairie homestead."

Rhinegold asked if it wasn't true some Snake Indians had been accused of eating white folks now and again.

So Longarm knew just how much Shoshoni scouting he'd likely done, despite his buckskin shirt and beat-up cavalry hat.

Longarm kept it polite, though, as he smiled thinly and told all of them, "The Indian nations come as different from one another as our own. A Shoshoni has no more in common with, say, a Mohawk than a Swede might have with a Turk. So whilst they do say a nation called Mohawk or Man Eaters might have deserved the compliment, the Shoshoni and all their Ho-speaking kin scare their kids silly with ghost stories about Piamuhmpitz, a big black cannibal owl bird who eats wicked children."

He took a drag on his cheroot and reached for his pocket watch as he continued. "I doubt Indians who ate folks would be so horrified at the notion of even an owl bird doing it, and even if Shoshoni had such disgusting habits, can anyone here see 'em sending all the way to Scotland for mail-order brides?"

The two women smiled. Old Angus never seemed to change his sour expression. Rhinegold shrugged and said, "Well, they do say some of the younger Shoshoni can read and write English, and ain't Pocatello in the flesh a Mormon convert?"

Longarm consulted his watch as he replied, "They say Geronimo is a Roman Papist, if that's supposed to mean anything. The Saints hold the American Indians to be lost tribes of Israel, in case you ever want to discuss such matters with a hostile coming at you, Mister Rhinegold. I'll ask Pocatello whether he sent away for any Mormon gals from Scotland as soon as I get up to Fort Hall, albeit I doubt he'll tell me he has. Meanwhile, I may be able to pick up Zion before that government bunch shows up, if they ever do."

He rose to his feet and headed for the back door to see where that breed kid might be with his damned dinnerware. Dame Flora got up to chase after him, saying she needed trail supplies as well, if she knew of a reasonable place to purchase any. She explained she and her party had run out south of the Idaho line, and that Angus had refused to let anyone take advantage of her at any of the widespread settlements they'd passed through since.

Longarm was too polite to say he'd been wondering why the four of them had been trying to buy breakfast at a stage stop if none of them had come in by stage. When he asked her where her riding and pack stock might be, she confirmed that, like him, they'd taken advantage of the only livery and wayside inn for a day's ride north or south. She said she wasn't used to sleeping on the ground and he believed her. They then saw that breed kid coming across the yard with Longarm's dinnerware in a fresh burlap sack. So Longarm gave the kid a cheroot, told him to leave the stuff inside by the stove, and asked if there might be a nearby general store that wasn't out to skin strange gentiles alive.

The kid said there was such a store out front and down the main street a ways to the south. He didn't know how they felt about the price of beans this far from the railroad. When Longarm said he'd passed the place riding in, and that there was only one way to find out, Dame Flora said she'd best not tell old Angus where they were headed.

Longarm didn't care. She seemed much better company than gloomy old Angus. As they circled the building wide she took his arm in a natural way, as if to confirm what he'd just told himself.

Chapter 7

The little frame store down the way was crammed to its
tin ceiling with everything from straight pins to moldboard
plows and penny candy to hundred-pound sacks of corn
meal. The little dried apple of a gent who ran the place
even kept coffee, tobacco, and racy reading material under
his counter for passing gentiles bound for the Montana
Territory. Dame Flora found their prices outrageous, but
Longarm told her the old cuss was being firm but fair,
explaining, "All the stuff from the outside world comes
in expensive, by packsaddle or freight wagon over many a
dusty bump, ma'am. You'll find local produce no more than
a few cents higher than in most country stores. Mormons
tithe a dime on the dollar to their temple after paying local
taxes. So I've seen higher prices out this way."

She said in that case it might be smarter to buy plenty of dry beans, bacon, and such in bulk. But Longarm
warned her, "Not if you mean to break camp every morning,
ma'am. I know you got servants to cook for you. But you
just don't have the time out on the trail."

He could see she wasn't used to doing her own cooking
as soon as she asked what he meant. The old storekeeper
cackled. "He knows a thing or two about beans, little lady.
So listen to him tight."

Longarm chuckled fondly and pointed at the piled sacks

of navy beans as he explained, "First you got to soak 'em in water at least twelve hours before you put 'em on the fire with mayhaps some sowbelly and molasses to simmer another six or eight, by which time I'd have eaten from cans and moved on at least twice. Folks in any hurry can ride quite a ways in even the time it takes a fresh spud to bake in the coals, come to study on it."

She still seemed undecided. So he asked just how much farther she and her own party meant to ride in search of other Scotch gals. When she frowned thoughtfully and said they'd probably ride on up to Fort Hall with him, Longarm smiled uncertainly and declared, "I ain't sure about that, ma'am. To begin with, it won't be for me to say once that government party catches up with us here. Even if they don't mind, I ain't sure you ought to. I've told you why I doubt those missing gals got lured anywhere by Shoshoni."

The old Mormon who ran the store had been doing his best to keep up with them. So he naturally asked if they were talking about new converts from the British Isles. When Dame Flora informed him they sure were, he told her, "This young jasper's right about that too. The Salt Lake Temple's written us to watch for such goings-on up at this end of the delta. Seems some kith or kin has gotten worried about an ugly young thing who got off the train at Ogden with a heap of cash and a lot of baggage. She'd told one of our own young ladies she'd met on the train about the big cattle baron she was on her way to marry up with. The sister she confided in said she had a lot of mighty queer notions about us Deseret folk."

Dame Flora anxiously questioned the old Mormon further while Longarm lifted down a case of canned sardines. He knew they were going to have to bring some pack brutes over to tote all this shit in the end, but meanwhile it made sense to eat the damned apple one bite at a time.

He was only half listening, because he'd known the old Mormon was going to inform Dame Flora that, no, they hadn't seen missing spinster gals here in Zion. A missing anything was by definition something nobody honest would have seen since it was first missed.

He had his own practical additions to his own supplies piled at one end of the counter by the time Dame Flora figured much the same and switched to buying her own much larger load. Longarm told them both he'd be right back to settle up with his own pack brute. He asked Dame Flora if she wanted him to haul old Angus and, say, a couple of her own pack brutes back with him. She dimpled at him a and said he was being awfully helpful. So he left her jawing about canned grub and lost, strayed, or stolen spinsters with the friendly old Mormon.

It only took him a few steps and a dozen drags on his smoke to make it back to the Overland station. But when he stepped inside to fetch Dame Flora's hired help, he found they'd been replaced near the potbellied stove by Buffalo Bill, Old Mother Hubbard, and maybe Pocahontas— or leastways, three odd-looking strangers dressed up like them.

On second glance the imposing white-haired gent in the white ten-gallon hat and matching fringed and beaded buckskins couldn't be the one and original William F. Cody, who'd only started acting so odd since he'd won that medal for killing Yellow Hand and taken to giving lectures about his misspent youth on the vaudeville circuit. This version of the Old Frontiersman rose to shake and introduce his foolish-looking self as the original Shoshoni Sam, whom Longarm had doubtless heard of. He introduced the motherly and sensibly dressed woman in the loose duster and poke bonnet as his wife, the famous tightrope-walker and bareback-rider Madame Marvella. The younger sort of gypsy-looking brunette, in a tailored but beaded and fringy outfit of wine red deerskin, was supposed to be a famous Indian princess named Tupombi, Princess Tupombi of that Comanche nation he'd doubtless heard of as well.

Longarm didn't feel up to insulting anyone who hadn't insulted him first. So he allowed he'd naturally heard of all of them, but that right now he was searching for some others who'd just been by that very stove. So Shoshoni Sam told him a gruff old Scotchman had told some scared little gal to go upstairs and pack something while he and a regular American went out back to see about their stock.

Longarm thanked him, explained that the sack of stuff on the floor was his, and picked it up as he added that old Angus and at least two pack brutes were needed by a lady down the way.

He was more bemused than annoyed when the Wild West apparition tagged along, confiding, "You may be just the man we've been hoping to meet up with. You did say you were a government man just now, did you not?"

Longarm agreed he'd introduced himself as Deputy U.S. Marshal Custis Long. So Shoshoni Sam said, "You must be the one they call Longarm. Us famous Westerners have to keep track of one another. I heard the government was up to something big with my Shoshoni blood brothers this fall. Might you be on your way up to Fort Hall?"

Longarm smiled crookedly and replied, "I might. Before we get even sillier, old son, hasn't anyone ever told you there's no such thing as a Comanche princess? The closest thing to royalty Indians had north of the Chihuahua Desert would have been the now-extinct Natchez Sun Clans, over by the Mississippi, and like I just said, they're extinct."

Shoshoni Sam said soothingly, "You know that and I know that, but what do the rubes care, and Tupombi really is Comanche. Part Comanche, I mean. Since confession may be good for the soul, I'll confess like a man that we're out here on the make for something big. No doubt you'll have heard of Phineas T. Barnum and his colored freak, Joice Heth, billed as the hundred-and-sixty-year-old wet nurse of George Washington?"

Longarm laughed lightly and said, "I have. She was a fake. The nurse died eight or ten years before I was born, at about the age of seventy or eighty."

Shoshoni Sam nodded and said, "You're right. But what would you say if I told you we were on the trail of the one and original genuine Sacajawea, the lovely Shoshoni maiden who led Lewis and Clark to glory and the wide Pacific Ocean?"

Longarm laughed less politely and replied, "I'd say you were a gent with a wry sense of humor. I was raised not to call my elders damned fools. For openers, and with all due respect, Sacajawea may have been Shoshoni. But after that she was no maiden. She was a woman grown with a papoose on her back, and we're talking about an expedition that took place a good seventy-five years ago!"

Then he spotted Rhinegold just inside the doorway of the stable ahead, and called out to him, telling Shoshoni Sam he was just too busy with important chores to speculate on circus freaks. When that didn't get rid of the pest, he sighed and said, "I wasn't at the funeral, but they give the year of Miss Sacajawea's death as 1812 on her grave marker over at Fort Union, Montana Territory, if you'd like to look it up. I only remembered because we got into a second war with the English that same year and one of my uncles had to do something about that under Jackson at New Orleans."

Rhinegold came out to meet them, with old Angus glowering out like an ogre from the doorway. So Longarm told the guide about all the supplies to be loaded down the way at the store, and as soon as Rhinegold said he'd see to it, Longarm went on in, with a nod at old Angus, to put a halter and packsaddle on his own roan.

Shoshoni Sam was still waiting out front as Longarm led the pony from the stable. It was commencing to get tedious, and Longarm said so when the buckskin-clad pest fell in step beside him afoot to declare, "I know they say Sacajawea died soon after she led the Lewis and Clark Expedition. But that tombstone at Fort Union is as brazen a hoax as George Washington's old nanny. Fort Union was only built in 1829, and *you* can look *that* up. So answer me how anyone by any name could have died there and been buried there in 1812?"

Longarm spied Dame Flora on the porch of the general store down the way and waved to her, telling Shoshoni Sam, "I don't have to. They've sent me out to hunt many an odd want in my time, but I'm pleased to report Miss Sacajawea ain't wanted nowhere, dead or alive."

As the two of them led the roan to the plank steps of the store Longarm felt obliged to present the freak-hunter to Dame Flora, unable to resist the chance to add, "He's searching for a missing lady as well, ma'am. A Shoshoni called Sacajawea. You might not have heard of her, being from Scotland and all, but should she turn up on the trail ahead try to make allowances for advanced years. I figure she'd be around a hundred or so by now."

Shoshoni Sam sounded serious as he insisted, "Princess Tupombi figures her younger than ninety-five, being she was in her teens as late as 1804, right?"

Dame Flora smiled uncertainly and replied, "If you say so, sir. How old might this Princess Tupombi be?"

Longarm sighed and said, "No more than twenty-odd, if she's even an Indian, ma'am. I should have mentioned Shoshoni Sam here is a professional showman. Meanwhile, Rhinegold ought to be here any minute with your own stock. So if you'll excuse me, I'd best go in and settle up my own transactions."

He did. The old Mormon sold him some extra coffee and the same brand of cheroots at *two*-for-a-nickel. But when Longarm asked if they had any Maryland Rye under the counter, the older man shot him a stern look and warned him not to press his gentile luck just because they were north of the Utah line.

Then old Angus came in, looking even sterner, to pick up the bags and boxes Dame Flora had already paid for. So getting all of it out that one door and aboard three pack ponies was a bit awkward, although not really tough.

Longarm didn't care if they finished ahead of him. He

wasn't aiming to ride on before those other government men showed up. But he was starting to care about that. He'd have never bulled on this far ahead of them if he'd known they were poking up along the trail in wheelchairs.

There was almost as much confusion getting both his and Dame Flora's fresh supplies under cover again at the Overland stop. A couple more stable hands had come back from breakfasts at home and either helped or added to the bustle, depending on who was fussing at whom.

Longarm was content to leave his recent purchases lashed to his packsaddle in their tack room. All his really expensive possibles were stored with his McClellan saddle under lock and key up in his hired room. His badge, identification, six-gun, money, and smokes he carried with him as usual, where it wouldn't matter whether anyone else had a passkey or not. But old Angus seemed certain there was a Mormon plot to steal every packet of salt and all the waterproof matches Longarm had advised his boss lady to buy. So he had those stable hands hopping as Longarm, already finished and getting tired of watching, got his McClellan and Winchester down from his own room and saddled the paint to do some scouting.

As he was leading it around to the front, afoot, that pesky Shoshoni Sam was standing there, smoking a two-bit claro. Longarm said, "Nice stock you got in there, if that was your matched bays and dapple gray I just admired a couple of stalls down from this scrub paint."

The showy showman cocked a bushy white brow at Longarm's mount to reply, "Oh, I wouldn't call the poor brute a scrub. I'd say it was more a barb and Irish hunter cross with at least one cayuse grandsire. Princess Tupombi would be a better judge of such stock. You can hardly beat a Comanche when it comes to judging horseflesh, you know."

Longarm dryly answered, "They do say that's the nation as first stole Spanish horseflesh way back when. Your tame Comanche looks a tad Irish too, come to study on it."

He forked himself aboard the paint before he added, "Now that we seem to have that settled, I got to get on down the road to see if I'll be wanting the hire of a room upstairs after the three o'clock check-out time they've posted on the inside of my door."

Shoshoni Sam said he didn't follow his drift. So Longarm hung around just long enough to say, "Back down the road a few hours' ride each way, while there's time. If I don't see any sign of the slowpokes I've been waiting on by noon or a tad later, I'll assume I'll still need that room tonight. Because even if they show up later this afternoon, at the rate they've been creeping, they'll surely want to bed down here for the night. This is about the last chance any of us will have for table meals and a lie-down under a real roof this side of Fort Hall."

Shoshoni Sam asked what sort of accommodations they might expect once they all got up to Fort Hall. Longarm said, "Not as fancy," and rode out. It would have taken too long to relate the history of Fort Hall to a buckskin-clad greenhorn, and in any case they'd all find out for themselves farther along.

So Longarm was inspired to chuckle and began to throw back his head and sing, at an easy trot . . .

Farther along, we'll know more about it.
Farther along, we'll understand why.
Cheer up, my brother.
Walk in the sunshine.
We'll understand it all, by and by.

Two young Mormon gals, hanging up washing in their railed-in yard, giggled and joined him in the next chorus without looking his way as he rode by. He knew they likely figured he was a Saint as well. There were times, over here in the delta, he almost wished he was. Both of them were pretty as pictures, and while they'd just started frowning on it at the Salt Lake Temple, a Saint could marry up with as many pretty gals as he felt up to supporting out in the Mormon countryside, where spoilsports weren't as likely to ruin the chances of Utah Territory becoming a full state of the Union.

He soon found himself singing alone again in the open country south of the modest settlement. For the first three miles, or about as far from his own doorstep as your average farmer wanted even his barley, the dirt road ran sunbaked between open fields and winding irrigation ditches. Irrigation had to accommodate to the lay of the land this close to the Wasatch Range to the east. But the stock pastures and open range further south offered more cover to anyone lurking within rifle range of the road. So Longarm heeled his mount to a thoughtful lope that might make him a tougher target even as it got him by each rocky outcrop or thick clump of new-growth timber sooner.

That was one of the worries left over from the first flush of pioneering. Once the country around a settlement had been scalped for timber and firewood, lots of second-growth weed trees tended to reclaim the parts nobody was using at the moment with thickets of stickerbrush and trashwood better for hiding in than anything else.

Second growth was good for birds, rabbits, and even deer, which inspired country folks who still hunted for the pot to cut back less of the barely useful shit. They'd left lots of aspen, he saw, with a few round autumn leaves still fluttering like gold coins in the least breeze, as if to keep anyone passing from spotting more sinister movement amid their closely packed trunks of greenish gray.

But once he'd put a good ten miles between himself and town, he began to feel better about the aspen and juniper clumps all about him on the open range that was now ungrazed. For despite more cover near the trail than he'd have tolerated had *he* been managing the Overland Line, the rolling country behind him was open enough for him to assume nobody was following him, and no matter how sore he'd made that whiskey-running bunch back yonder, he'd only told one greenhorn, an outsider, where he might be headed.

There seemed no way on earth for anyone with a guilty conscience to be laying for the law by the trail ahead, and thus Longarm was as astonished as alarmed when he topped a rise to see a flash of sunlight on metal amid some aspen flutter ahead. He rolled out of his saddle, Winchester and all, just as a high-powered round beat the report of its express rifle through the shallow gap between the cantle and swells of an already battered army saddle.

That rifle round would have surely done more damage to Longarm's left hip than the sunbaked dirt did to his right one when he hit it with his carbine butt as well and rolled away into the shin-deep grass on the west side of the trail.

He did that because the son of a bitch who'd just tried to dry-gulch him was firing some more from those aspen over to the east of the trail.

As his paint turned tail and ran back toward town with its eyes rolling and reins dragging, Longarm saw his unseen enemy hadn't been trying to kill him. He'd simply spooked the pony for a better shot at his intended target. Longarm knew this for certain when that distant rifle spanged again and his poor hat, which he'd parted company with on the way down, soared skyward amid shattered straw and dirt clods to his left. He knew his real position had to be hidden better by the tall dry grass all around. He was already prone with his elbows spread and his Winchester cocked and aimed the right general direction. So he held on to his edge by not even breathing hard enough to stir the springy stems above him.

A million years crept by. Then a distant voice called out to him, "We see you there, stranger! Stand up with your hands polite and tell us what you're doing in these parts!"

Longarm did no such thing. Assholes who fired on any-one using a public right of way in broad day could hardly be trusted not to gun another asshole who gave them such a swell chance.

The same voice called out, "I swear we'll open fire if you ain't on your feet by the time I counts to ten!"

So Longarm waited as the cuss in those trees to his east counted aloud, then fired again and again in the general direction his poor old hat had been headed. Longarm figured from the rate of fire that the rascal had a single-shot breech-loading .51 without a scope sight. He was firing too blind at the limit of his effective aim. Those awesome express rounds would kill at over a mile if they hit, but in practice an average shot was doing better than average if he could hit anything at three hundred yards.

Judging by the sun dazzle he'd spotted just in time, Longarm had the range figured at more like five hundred, which was another good reason to keep his own peace with the grass stems all around. He knew that even if he'd been able to see the son of a bitch, his Winchester's effective range was two hundred. So he had to get a good bit closer, or the asshole would have to get closer to *him,* before it would be a fair fight.

Another voice, a tad further south, bawled, "Cut wasting that expensive shot and ball, Pearly. I think he's already hit."

The high-powered rifle spanged again before the original rascal called back, "He'd better be, now that you've yelt my name to the four winds, you stupid kid!"

The stupid kid yelled back, "Aw, shit, I'll go look if you're too yeller-bellied, Pearly."

The one who seemed to be called Pearly called back, "Don't you dast! That ain't no ragged-ass sheepherder over yonder, kid. Pappy told us not to take no chances with *this* old boy, and he'd skin me alive if I was to get *you* kilt instead."

The one called Kid digested that, then called, "Well, we can't just wait here like sparrow birds on a telegraph wire till someone else comes riding along, can we?"

Longarm didn't see why not. But nobody was asking him. So he offered no suggestions as he lay there, dying for a smoke.

A grasshopper landed on the barrel of his Winchester and began to wash its front legs with tobacco juice spit, as if to tease a poor soul forced to do without as the sun rose ever higher. Longarm muttered, "Just you wait, Bug. We'll be having our first frost most any morning now at this altitude, and you know what the ant warned you grasshoppers about in that old tale by Mister Aesop."

The grasshopper paid him no mind. So he knew he was holding as still as he needed to. Critters always noticed movement before a human might. The older of the humans responsible for this dumb fix bawled out, "Come back here, you fool kid! We can't even be sure where he landed in all that deep grass!"

So Longarm knew what was headed his way long before the grasshopper near his front sight suddenly spooked and went whirring off on wings of black and gold. Longarm simply raised the sight until it was aimed at blue sky just above the amber tips of the screening grass. Sure enough, a tall gray hat preceded a tanned moronic face into Longarm's dead aim, to wind up dead and in point of fact sort of messy as Longarm blasted away point-blank while the dumb jaw commenced to drop at the sight of its own impending demise.

As the kid's shattered skull jerked backwards from under its big gray hat Longarm was already rolling sideways. So he wasn't at all where he had been when that more careful as well as more distant rifleman fired sensibly but too late at the haze of gunsmoke left by Longarm's deadlier shot.

When Longarm saw the rascal was aiming at the moving grass tips above him he froze on his belly again, but gripped his Winchester by its warm muzzle to reach as far away as he could with the butt plate, and then rolled it through the grass in apparent agony as he wailed, "Oh, shit, I give! I give! You got me bad and I need a doc!"

The one called Pearly bawled, "I'll give you one, you fucker! Are you still with us, Kid?"

Neither Longarm nor the one he'd just shot replied, of course, as Pearly shot the shit out of nothing much where Longarm had been rolling that butt plate about. He had it back in place against his right shoulder by the time Pearly let up, called again to his sidekick, and then wailed, "Aw, shit, Pappy ain't gonna like the way this turned out at all! Come on, Kid, quit funning me and say you only ducked, all right?"

Longarm just lay low.

Another million years later he heard hoofbeats, two ponies moving off on the far side of those aspen judging from the echoes all around.

Longarm still lay low. He'd played the same old Indian trick in his time. It was an old Indian trick because it had worked so many times.

The sun got high as it ever went and began to roll down the west slope of the clear autumn sky. Despite the altitude and his recent promise to that grasshopper, Longarm was really commencing to despise President Hayes and the reforms that called for damned old frock coats the damned sun could bake a man in as if he was a damned potato wrapped in damp adobe. For if it was true old U.S. Grant had been asleep at the switch while his crooked cronies had robbed him and the rest of the country blind, at least a federal deputy had been able to get by in no more than a shirt and vest back then, as long as he combed his damned hair now and again.

There was no safe way to roll out of his tweed coat without a grass stem or more giving away this new position. As if to prove that, he heard those damned ponies coming back, or leastways, he heard two ponies coming at a trot, sounding more as if they were on that dirt road just a few yards off. But Longarm never let on he might still be alive until he heard someone rein in and call out in a female voice, "Is

83

that you I see with one hand out on the roadway, Deputy Long?"

He stayed put but risked calling back, "Not hardly, ma'am. I suspicion you're looking at someone I just shot, and watch those aspen over to your left as you dismount on my side Indian-style."

The unseen gal laughed harshly and allowed she always did. So Longarm wasn't too surprised when he propped himself up on one elbow for a better look at the so-called Princess Tupombi. She was already demurely afoot in her garish cigar-store-Indian outfit, holding the leads of her dapple gray and his roan cayuse. He figured out why his saddle was aboard the roan instead of the paint before she called out, "Are you hurt? When your pony came back without you I thought it best to come looking for you with a less-jaded mount."

Nobody seemed to be shooting at either of them at the moment. So Longarm got gingerly to his feet and headed her way, calling a mite softer with a brighter smile, "That was mighty considerate of you with old Tanapah really feeling his oats this afternoon."

It didn't trip her up as planned. The pretty little thing gave a happy gasp and proceeded to give him what for in Ho, despite her big blue eyes and more Celtic than Comanche features.

Longarm laughed sheepishly and stopped her as he began to shuck his coat without letting go of his Winchester. "Hold your fire, ma'am. I know Tanapah is the sun father, that *ayee* means yes and *ka* means no. But after that I don't know much more Ho than any other Saltu."

She sighed and said, "My mother's people call your kind Taibo more often. Who's that Taibo sprawled in the grass over there?"

Longarm said, "I'm still working on that. I thought Saltu was the proper word for stranger, Princess."

She explained, "Saltu is *a* word, not *the* word. Don't you call a Mexican a dago as well as a greaser?"

He cocked a brow and replied, "I get along with 'em best by referring to 'em as Mexicans. I take it Taibo is a tad worse than Saltu."

To which she demurely replied, "Of course. Didn't they tell you my mother's people were Penataka?" and he silently chalked that up as another point in her favor.

He had it on good authority that the Penataka or Honey Eaters were the biggest and hence most common Comanche clan. A show-off with a fair grasp of Indian lore might have been more tempted to claim membership in the smaller but more celebrated Kwahadi, who'd ridden to glory under Quanah at Adobe Walls and in other noisy shindigs.

He was commencing to feel she might be only half fake. Buffalo Bill was half fake these days, yet he really had killed Yellow Hand and all those buffalo before he'd taken to dressing so odd and bragging on things he'd never done.

Longarm took the reins of his roan from her with a grateful nod and lashed his rolled tweed coat behind his McClellan as he tersely brought her up to date on his recent misadventures. She followed afoot, leading her bare-backed gray by the single line of her rawhide hackamore or bitless bridle. He'd already noted how Quill Indian she rode, despite the odd coloration of her eyes and deerskin duds. His bit-led roan commenced to fuss as he led it closer to the scent of fresh-spilled blood. He whacked its muzzle just enough to gain its undivided attention, and got them all a mite closer before he turned to ask the pretty breed, "Would you mind both brutes again just a minute or so? I see where my hat landed now, and we'll want this dead one lashed facedown across my saddle as well."

"Speak for yourself," she said in with a wrinkle of her tawny pug nose, adding, "He tried to kill you. Let him rot. I'll help you drag him further from the road if you're concerned about the few who may come this way before the carrion crows have had a good meal of bad Taibo."

He moved off through the deep grass to retrieve his

capsized Stetson and put it back on before he explained on the way back to her, "I'd like to have others look him over before the crows eat what's left of his fool face. I seem to have upset a white-trash clan back in Zion and this jasper and his sidekick made mention of someone they called Pappy, who seemed to want me dead. Personal. If this poor soul turns out to have been named Robbins, I can work out his pappy from there. Easy."

With the pretty breed minding the ponies he hunkered down to go through the dead man's duds, adding, "If nobody in Zion can identify him I'll have a bigger wonderment on my plate and . . . Hello, I see he took out a library card in San Antone one time. Outlaws do that a heap. But I doubt his name was really Miles Standish. Albeit his hat over yonder reads sort of Texas as well and . . . Yep, I sure want the folks in an Idaho county seat to look this cuss over before he starts to spoil."

She helped mostly by holding Longarm's Winchester and soothing both ponies as Longarm manhandled the still-limp body up over and facedown across his McClellan. As he was lashing the cadaver securely in place with latigo strips, she observed he seemed to have a knack for such gruesome tasks. To which he could only modestly reply he'd had some practice.

She said, "I'll bet you have. You are the lawman my Ute cousins call Saltu Ka Saltu, aren't you?"

He shrugged and said, "I reckon. I arrested a mucky-muck with the B.I.A. who'd been held over from Grant's Indian Ring one time, and the Utes seemed to find that sort of astounding."

"The stranger who is not a stranger," she mused with a sort of Mona Lisa smile. "I can see why they were astounded. My father was Scotch-Irish, and a decent man, but you people fucked the Utes above and beyond the call of duty, after they'd helped you round up the Navajo back in the sixties."

Longarm winced and replied, "I wish you wouldn't say

86

anybody helped me personally round anybody up. That was Kit Carson they sent after wayward Navajo that time, and Carson himself complained to Washington when the B.I.A. under Grant let the Indian Ring get a few Ute leaders drunk and grabbed all that land out from under the whole nation. Do you reckon that gray of your own would be able to carry the both of us at a trot, Princess Tupombi?"

She said, "He'll have to, unless one of us means to ride atop a dead man or walk that far. I wish you'd stop calling me Princess, by the way. I'm not even the *porivo* my mother was. But no matter how often I try to explain that to Shoshoni Sam he keeps insisting nobody would understand what a *porivo* was and that princess seems close enough."

Longarm chuckled and took the reins so she could vault lightly up on her gray, to land astride as well as bareback, giving him quite a view of her long tawny legs.

It wouldn't have been polite to ask if she was wearing any underdrawers. So he just forked aboard behind her, holding the lines of both ponies in his left fist as he swung the Winchester around her slim waist to ride across her lap, with his gun hand still gripping the action. His right wrist fit into the nice angle formed by her trim pelvis and widespread right thigh as if it belonged there.

She didn't argue about that, but warned him she'd better hold the lead pony's single rein. He let her, even though it meant a left fist down against his own less interesting hip as he asked her which of them ought to heel the critter's ribs.

She said, "Neither. This one's Penataka bred and broken. He'll buck if anyone tries to abuse him Taibo-style."

She proved that by clucking softly to the gray. The next thing Longarm knew they were moving out at an easy mile-eating trot he should have found ball-breaking with no stirrups to stand in, but didn't, thanks to the smooth gait and springy spine of the pony.

It wasn't true all Indians were natural cavalry generals,

any more than it was true every Russian wood-carver had the makings of a Cossack. Some nations would as soon eat a horse as get on one, and as dangerous as Lakota could be coming at you at full gallop, they still called their mounts *tashunkas,* or big dogs, and tended to be rougher on them than green cavalry troopers because they set great store in *stealing* the horses they rode, and thus had little time to waste on breaking them gently.

Other nations, the Cayuse in particular and the Comanche, Shoshoni, and Utes in general, tended to baby the ponies they bred, as well as stole, with a mighty good eye for horseflesh. So they tended to ride the ideal Indian pony of Ned Buntline's Wild West Romances, and this dapple gray he was riding with a lady in wine-red Indian duds was a swell pony, even by Comanche standards. When she modestly denied breaking it herself, they established she'd been educated as white as the white kids of the boarding school her Indian trading pop had sent her to would let her act. She'd been baptized Mary Jo, but took an adult Indian name, as Indians got to, once she'd run home to her momma. Tupombi meant no more than Brunette, which got less odd when you considered her Comanche kin had allowed her to choose it, and that the white kids at that boarding school had been inclined to call her Nigger. She said a *porivo,* which her momma had been, translated more as a woman who was allowed to be heard with as much respect as a *powamu,* or important man with medicine, than a regal title such as Shoshoni Sam had suggested.

He said he savvied some of the more open customs of Ho-speaking folk who shook their feathered *pahos* at Taiowa, the Great Creative Mystery. When she told him she could see he really *had* been paying attention, he felt bold enough to ask, "So what's all this nonsense about asking Sacajawea of the Lewis and Clark Expedition to join a Wild West Show at this late date?"

Tupombi said, "It's not nice to call a story nonsense before you've heard it. The one I'm sure they told *you,* in your own Taibo schoolbooks, is pretty silly in its own right."

He asked how so, even as he tried to recall the little he'd read and heard about old-timers who'd died before he'd been born. The pretty little thing sort of riding in his lap began with, "That name they put down as her real one was awfully dumb. She was a Shoshoni girl, captured by Minnetaree Hidasta and sold to a metís or half-breed French Canadian that Lewis and Clark soon hired for a guide. His name was Charbonneau. He is not important to my true story of Boinaiv."

Longarm frowned and said, "Lewis and Clark didn't think much of old Charbonneau, who seemed to know less about the mountains ahead than his pretty young squaw. But who was this Boinaiv?"

She sounded impatient as she answered, "The one everyone keeps calling Sacajawea, of course. Her real name, Boinaiv, means Daughter of Grass. I don't know the vision that inspired that. When Boinaiv cried so much because she'd been captured and taken east across the Shining Mountains, her captors, not any Ho-speakers, started to call her Bird Woman, or Sakaka Wea, as you'd say that in their Sioux way. Sacajawea means nothing sensible in Ho."

Longarm thought and decided, "By gum, *wihaw* does sound the way Lakota and such refer to their womenfolk. They don't like it when you call 'em squaws. But hold on, I do recall reading somewhere about Sacajawea meaning something about canoes in her own native lingo."

Tupombi snorted. "A bird woman riding in a canoe being pulled? Some so-called Indian scholars have tortured Sacajawea into such Shoshoni baby talk, and Shoshoni Sam keeps saying nobody will ever pay a dime to meet anyone called Grass Baby, and I fear he may be right. I only agreed to help him and Miss Marvella to find Boinaiv. I owe them for getting me out of a fix a lot like the one the crying Boinaiv found herself in when Lewis and Clark came along. I was stranded in Kansas City when the owner of an other Wild

West Show decided he didn't like my stuck-up-ways. Then the manager of my hotel insisted on being paid or taking it out in trade, in bed with me."

Longarm grimaced and said, "That's how come mothers warn their daughters about show folk, ma'am. But even assuming way nicer show folk took you under their wing and asked you to help 'em track down a more famous Indian lady, what in thunder makes you think a gal who marched over the mountains with Lewis and Clark back in the days of the first Napoleon, as a woman grown, would still be—"

"Somewhere in her nineties," Tupombi cut in. "She was in her early teens, pregnant or not, when she led the way west back in 1804. But there's more to it than the mere fact it would be possible for most any healthy person to live to be a hundred or more. If you know my mother's tongue at all you know the people you call Snakes and Comanche are really one. So both nations tell the same tale of a proud Ho woman leaving the breed brute who beat her and his other Indian wives. They say that to avoid Charbonneau and other Taibo mountain men who might have helped him she rode far south, far, to fall in with the Quohada or Antelope People you also know as a Comanche band. They say an important *powamu* made her his paramount wife because she was not only beautiful but knew so many secrets of both his red and white enemies. I cannot tell you his name because nobody knows it now. You know how my mother's people are about the names of those who have gone back to Taiowa."

Longarm nodded soberly and observed, "Makes the true history of you all a chore to figure too. But we can still talk about Bird Woman because she's still supposed to be alive?"

Tupombi nodded the back of her head to him but said, "She was given that name by enemies. I know you find this hard to understand. Shoshoni Sam finds it impossible because he understands no Ho at all. He keeps trying to say things to me in baby-talk Algonquin. He thinks squaw, papoose, and moccasin are Shoshoni words."

Longarm said, "Well, he does call himself Shoshoni Sam. What makes you think Sacajawea or, all right, Boinaiv would be way up at Fort Hall, dead or alive, if she was last seen married to a Comanche chief down around the Staked Plains?"

Tupombi said, "I just told you her man was turned into a ghost nobody remembers much about. They think it might have been in a bad fight with Taibo, whether Mexican or Anglo, back when everyone was fighting for control of West Texas. By this time Boinaiv wasn't afraid of her French Canadian man anymore, and before she'd run away from him they'd had a son, a healthy one with a lot of *puha*, who'd been sent to a fine school by the red-headed chief, William Clark."

Longarm brightened and said, "Oh, sure, I know about John Baptiste Clark Chapineau, better known as Pomp and born along the way to the wide Pacific. Wasn't there some scandalized gossip at the time about old Clark giving the lad his name as a middle name after being so friendly with his Shoshoni mamma?"

Tupombi shrugged and sounded unconcerned as she replied, "He could have fucked her had he wanted to. That was one of the reasons she and a dozen or so other Indian girls had been brought along. But Pomp Chapineau was almost surely the son of her half-breed lord and master because she was carrying when the two of them joined the expedition. Do you want to hear my story or do you want to talk dirty about a girl who had no say at all in the matter?"

He said, "Well, Clark never would have named that Judith Basin after a gal waiting for him back home if he hadn't been sort of fond of her as well. Keep talking about Sacajawea-Boinaiv and her long-lost mixed-breed son. Didn't he die of Rocky Mountain spots during the Montana gold rush, around '66?"

She sighed and replied, "Some say it was water on the lungs. I told you my mother's people don't like to talk about ghosts. I don't know whether Boinaiv ever met her grown son again when the two of them were seen around the Montana gold fields about the same time. I hope she did, and that he was kind to her. In any case she was last seen back north, in Shoshoni country where she belonged."

"Back up and study on an old lady searching for a middle-aged son just after a war betwixt the states that's already commencing to fade into legend," he said. "Even if she survived the shock of her breed son's death, you've still got her in Montana Territory, on the wrong side of the Divide for Fort Hall. So what's the sense of searching for her on the Fort Hall reserve when she belongs at the Wind River Agency with the Eastern Shoshoni?"

They could see Mormon cows grazing all about by this time as they kept riding in, with Tupombi explaining, "To begin with, she doesn't belong with the eastern bands. She was born and raised a West Shoshoni of the Agaiduka band. After that, she wouldn't be at the Wind River Agency, dead or alive. Shoshoni Sam wired Fort Washakie over a month ago, when I first told him the story."

Longarm frowned at the kissable back of her tawny neck as he silently digested that. It would have been impolite to suggest a Wild West gal who'd been stranded in a K.C. hotel might make up an even wilder story if she felt she had to.

Chapter 8

The dead gunslick was a mite stiff and grinning like a shit-eating dog by the time they got him into town. From the way some of the townsfolk gaped one might think they'd never seen a white man riding double with a pretty Indian and leading a cadaver on another pony before.

Longarm unloaded the one he'd nailed on the sunny side of the modest country courthouse, where the afternoon warmth could sort of thaw a bowed body into a more dignified position on the grass. Tupombi said she'd carry both ponies back to the Overland stop and see to their proper care. He said he'd join her and the others there as soon as he compared notes on the one called The Kid with the local law.

That didn't take long. Tupombi and the ponies were barely out of view before a morose old cuss wearing a gray Abe Lincoln beard and gilt county badge elbowed through the growing crowd in a suit less dusty than Longarm's. The younger federal lawman had naturally pinned his own silver badge to his tweed vest before riding anywhere worth mentioning in the company of a gunshot victim.

The county deputy introduced himself as Bishop Reynolds. So Longarm knew he took his law-enforcement duties less seriously than your average political appointee. The stern-faced Mormon lawman paid close attention, however, as Longarm filled him in on why he'd just deposited a dead man on the grounds of the Zion County Courthouse. The Kid was still grinning foolishly with what was left of his face from, say, the eye sockets down, but as Longarm had hoped, he was commencing to lie straighter now. An undertaking gal who'd baked him a swell cactus pie one time had explained that temporary stiffness to him, and told him how they dealt with it in her trade.

As Bishop Reynolds dropped to one knee and began to fumble with the dead man's buttons Longarm said, "He ain't one of your own. He wore his hat with a Texas crease, packed doubtless-fake Texican identification, and as you can see now, wore red flannel underwear."

Bishop Reynolds left the dead man's shirtfront half ajar as he grimly observed, "I thought he was a gentile. Tell me more about the trouble you had with Pete Robbins and his godless litter."

Longarm smiled thinly and observed, "News sure travels, even when it ain't got far to go. But I didn't have that much trouble with the timid cuss who serves grub to white travelers and redeye to red locals. They seem to have simply lit out as soon as I told 'em I was a federal lawman who couldn't be bought off."

He nudged the gentile he'd brought in with a thoughtful boot tip as he added, "I didn't expect them to take things this seriously. It was my impression we were talking about nothing more sinister than swapping trade liquor for wild game and vegetables. Anyone making a habit of that ought to know the federal government may frown on trading redeye to its reservation wards, but doesn't get excited unless you start distilling it untaxed as well."

Bishop Reynolds got back to his feet, muttering, "Where did you think Pete Robbins *got* his corn liquor, from *us*? The Salt Lake Temple has enjoined us to obey the law of the land, which is why you see me wearing this badge to enforce the temporal laws of Deseret."

"No offense, but this ain't Utah Territory," Longarm said, as respectfully as the occasion seemed to call for.

The church elder and deputy sheriff sniffed and said, "I still take my serious commandments from our Salt Lake Temple, and before you start up about that, I'd best advise you Salt Lake defines the law of the land as those provisions and only those provisions of the U.S. Constitution *all* of us must abide by. There's not one word in the federal constitution that requires any state or territorial government to license any liquor distillery, so . . ."

"Pete Robbins is a moonshiner," Longarm finished, staring soberly down at the one called The Kid. "I can see how a cuss with an illicit still out in the nearby hills might have more to worry about than sneak-swapping a jug someone else made for a side of venison now and again. But how do you reckon they knew where to lie in wait for me so far south of town? I only told one gent, and him a stranger here as well, I was heading out to see what might have bogged that government party down."

Old Reynolds glanced about, as if to make sure all the faces in the fair-sized crowd were on his side before he cautiously confided, "You couldn't have passed anyone Pete Robbins had any business with if you rode directly south."

Longarm cautiously asked, "Meaning we might be talking about a home spread to the east, west, or north, with or without its own sweet scent of sour mash?"

Reynolds shook his head and replied, "We're talking about this other gentile you've deposited dead on our courthouse grass. My duties to your kind do not include your bad habits. I frankly see little or no difference between a man smoking or drinking stimulants himself and tempting others, red or white, to do the same."

Longarm nodded, but demanded, "Do you take as casual an attitude about an already lost sinner trying to dry-gulch a federal lawman within the fuzzy outlines of your theocracy, Bishop Reynolds?"

The older man shook his head no, but pointed out, "There's not one shred of evidence connecting this total stranger with any of our local folk, Saint or sinner."

Longarm started to say something dumb. Then he nodded grudgingly. "You're right. This one's not about to confess any other motive, but that's not saying he couldn't have had one. Just before I got him instead, I heard his pard call him The Kid. That pard would seem to have answered to Pearly, and they were both out to get me at the behest of someone called Pappy. I don't suppose that means much to anyone here?"

Reynolds said it didn't, and turned to the others all around for any light they could shed on the subject. But nobody there had heard of a Zion County rider called Pearly. So many riders answered to Kid that nobody wanted to jaw about a Kid none of them had ever seen before. More than one Mormon townsman confirmed that Miss Zelda at the Overland stop called her uncle, Pete Robbins, most anything but Pappy. Even her half-witted kid brother, another kid entirely, seemed to fathom the difference between a pappy and an uncle.

Longarm asked more questions, and soon made a deal with ambitious locals in exchange for the contents of the dead man's wallet along with his guns, fair watch, and silver-mounted spurs.

A Mormon druggist who doubled as a part-time undertaker said he could tidy the cadaver up enough for a gentile photographer to record his dead features for future reference. After that, there'd be just enough time left over to plant him, unembalmed but wrapped in a tarp almost good as new over in Potter's Field, beyond the town dump.

By this late in the afternoon they all had to concern themselves with the remaining daylight. So as the druggist and his hired help got cracking with the cadaver, Longarm took the older lawman aside to say he'd be at the Overland stop at least one more night, if anyone more important wanted him to sign anything.

Reynolds sniffed, pointed out he'd already told Longarm he was the local *bishop,* for land's sake, and said he'd send a boy over to get that squaw's signature as well, once he'd

96

had time to write a proper report for the country records. So they shook and parted friendly, with Longarm feeling fairly sincere. For despite some of the fine print in that Book of Mormon, he had to respect folks who went by what they said they stood for.

Most everybody said they considered women human beings, and most everyone who'd never had any kith or kin scalped just gushed about that noble savage, Mister Lo. But Bishop Reynolds acted as if the *signed deposition* of a female Indian was worth taking the time and trouble to record.

As he strode the short but dusty distance to the Overland stop Longarm reflected on how well Mormons seemed to get along with both their womenfolk and Indian neighbors. The Angel Moroni had told them the American Indians were one or more of the Lost Tribes of Israel. So instead of calling them damned diggers and shooting them on sight, the way more sensible Saltu might, the Saints had tried to convert them or, failing that, make friends with them at least.

Longarm didn't ascribe the sinister motives others might to the Mormon Indian policy. He'd always found it easier to share tobacco smoke instead of gunsmoke with any Indian who'd meet him halfway. So he doubted it was true *all* Indian attacks in and about the Great Basin had been instigated by murderous Mormon missionaries, although there had been that massacre at Mountain Meadows, and the army must have had *some* evidence against Brother Lee and those other Mormons they hung that time for attacking that wagon train and blaming it on Indians.

He found a friendlier-looking Indian, with big blue eyes, out front as he approached the Overland stop. Tupombi said, "What have you been doing all this time? I was about to come looking for you. Those Scotch people have ridden on, with night about to fall and a chance of snow in the cold wind's breath."

Longarm sniffed, didn't smell anything but sage after a long sunny day, and replied, "Do tell? Well they got a Great

Basin man guiding 'em and a half-moon rising. Did they say what inspired 'em to light out alone after all? Dame Flora told me earlier how much she wanted to tag along with that bigger government party."

Tupombi said, "The *porivo* with flaming hair said she was tired of waiting, waiting, and wanted to use the talking wire the army must have up at Fort Hall."

Longarm frowned thoughtfully. "Rhinegold hired on as a man who knows this country and he's expecting an army telegraph at Fort Hall?"

Tupombi nodded. "They do have a telegraph at both Fort Hall and Fort Washakie. Shoshoni Sam wired both forts to ask about Boinaiv, or Sacajawea. They said they'd heard she died a long time ago. So there must be two army forts, no?"

Longarm shook his head. "No. There's a small army garrison at Fort Washakie, on the far side of the Divide. Fort Hall was the grand notion of a fur trader called Wyeth. He built it as a trading post on the Snake River back in the shining times of the beaver hat craze. The Hudson Bay Company from up Canada way bought Wyeth out back around '36 because he'd picked such a swell location."

"Then why did they call it a fort?" she demanded with her female logic.

Longarm smiled down at her to explain, "Same reasons they called Bent's private fort on the Arkansas a fort. Because it was built as a fort, of course. No offense, but some of your momma's kin have a time grasping our notions of property rights, and the trade goods a trader might have on hand are generally picked with demand on the part of the consumer in mind."

She said, "Oh. Then those Scotch people are going to have to pay to use the telegraph wire from a trading post? Good. I told them it was a bad time to push on into disputed country alone, and your Dame Flora spoke to me as if I was a child."

Longarm shrugged and said, "She ain't my Dame nothing and she talks that way to most everybody. I take it you, Shoshoni Sam, and Madame Marvella mean to wait some more for that lost, strayed, or stolen column of dudes I just can't account for?"

She said they were, that the station manager had agreed to let the well-traveled Madame Marvella rustle up some supper in the kitchen if she'd show his Lulu how it was done, and that her own dear momma had never taught her to prepare food in the Taibo fashion and that she wasn't interested in learning.

He chuckled and confided he'd always ducked mess duty in his army days as often as he could. When she said her mentor, Shoshoni Sam, had been smoking inside by the stove a few minutes ago, Longarm chuckled fondly and suggested, "What say we let him smoke alone, lest he feel inspired to teach you a useful trade? When I was in the army I found that out of sight was out of mind. So I tried to avoid showing up for anything less important than pay call, mail call, mess call, and such. Why don't we mosey back down to that general store and give Madame Marvella and Lulu time to set the table inside? I feel certain Shoshoni Sam or the station manager will holler for us before our grub gets too cold."

She fell in step beside him as he flung his coat over one shoulder but left his gun hand free. When she asked what they might be after at the store ahead he explained, "Nothing. They'll likely be fixing to close for the night. Meanwhile, they got front steps just made for watching the road south as old Tanapah calls it a day in the west."

She took it wrong. She pouted, "Don't mock my *puha*, even if you think it's sort of silly. My father's people tried to convince me I should shake *paho* at a weakling who'd allowed his enemies to nail him to a cross without fighting them, and I thought *that* was sort of silly too!"

He motioned at the store steps they could see ahead now as he soberly replied, "Your boys don't fight when the *ahotey* is skewering 'em to do some sun dancing either, speaking of odd religious notions, and having witnessed more sun dances than I ever wanted to, I'm sure I'd as soon be crucified if I just had to choose one or the other."

She insisted it wasn't the same. Men could be like that when you argued religion with them too. So he said soothingly "Let's just say I only meant the sun was mighty low in the west and talk of things that might have answers, such as how high could up go or how long might forever last."

She laughed and confessed she'd never figured those puzzles out either. They saw the general store had been shuttered against the gathering dusk as they sat down on the warm plank steps. But Longarm decided not to reach for a smoke in such a public place, with or without any Mormons in sight.

Tupombi locked her tawny fingers around her upraised although modestly skirted knees as she leaned back, saying, "The sunset is beautiful, no matter who or what is painting the clouds so many colors, many. You were telling me why Fort Hall is not an army post. Is it still a trading post?"

He thought before he went on. "Well, there's a trading post to be found there, across from the Indian agency and such. Think of it more as a sprawl that busted out of its original stockade back in wagon train days before the war. Sited as it was, where the Oregon Trail met the Shake River, Fort Hall might have grown into as big a town as Fort Boise, another Hudson Bay trading post over to the west. But it never did, because it was handier to the strongholds of the Bannock-Shoshoni bands that worried travelers along the Oregon Trail whether they did anything worrisome or not."

Tupombi sighed and said, "We heard about the army killing all those men, women, and children near the big bend of the Bear River. It seemed very cruel to us."

Longarm stared off into the sunset as he quietly replied, "Well, some of us took some *Indian* pranks sort of serious as well. I'd as soon argue religion as figure out who first did what, to whom, with what, Miss Tupombi. Can't we forget the self-seeking tales told by mean rascals on both sides and

100

agree most folk, red and white, act about as decent as others might let 'em?"

She said it was easier for him to say, adding, "You don't know the bad things, many bad things, some of your people have done."

He shook his head. "You're wrong. I still got this fool badge pinned to my vest and I've been toting it six or eight years now. I won't offend your Comanche ears with half the tales of blood and slaughter I could fill 'em with. So suffice it to say I've seen lots of bad things done to folks, red and white, by human monsters, or just plain folks, as red or white. Folks can sure act scary when they're scared of one another."

She agreed it might be friendlier to gossip about less blood-thirsty topics. He said he had no idea whether Dame Flora or her maid, the plainer but sort of shapely Jeannie, took care of the gruff but rather virile-looking Angus after dark. She said she'd walked in on Shoshoni Sam and Madame Marvella in the middle of a crime against nature. But he told her he didn't want to hear about it before she could say just what they'd been up to, or down on.

He was sorry he'd gotten her off the subject of the older couple as soon as she shifted her attention from their private lives to his own. Most gals he met seemed content to learn he wasn't married up or seriously spoken for. But Tupombi wanted to know how he satisfied his natural feelings if he didn't have any lady friends.

He told her a deputy on duty in the field just had to grin and bear it, unless he got lucky. So she naturally asked if he thought it really changed a man's luck if he dallied with ladies of color.

He laughed, sort of red-eared, and allowed he'd seldom heard a Comanche breed described as a lady of color. Which inspired her to blush even harder and protest she hadn't been suggesting any such thing.

Before he could ask what she *had* been suggesting with all this suggestive talk, they both heard the thunder of hooves and rattle of wheel rims and tie rods to the south. So they turned as one to spy the Overland stage coming in, fast, through the gathering dusk.

The six-mule team hauled the swaying Concord coach past them at full gallop. Neither the driver nor shotgun man seemed to pay much attention to anything around them. As Longarm and Tupombi watched the rear boot of the coach fade north behind all that dust, Tupombi observed they'd come in as if Quanah Parker, in the flesh and wearing paint, was right behind them.

Longarm got to his feet and held out a hand to help her do the same as he replied, "Great minds run in the same channels. I was about to say supper could be almost ready by now, and either way, that coach just came up the trail that missing government team was supposed to be following."

As they legged it back to the Overland stop faster than they'd left it, Tupombi brightened and said, "Oh, I see. You want to ask the coach crew whether they passed your friends on the trail or not."

Longarm sighed and replied he'd just said that. He knew why she was talking so much and saying so little. He'd once caught himself being sort of windy in the company of a gal he really wanted, before he'd learned it was a dead giveaway and more likely to spoil a good chance than advance it. Women of experience, the best kind to experience, were inclined to shy at would-be lovers who came at them acting sort of silly. He'd learned to be wary of silly gals for the same practical reasons. The game was confusing enough when you played it with other sensible grown-ups.

Indians were not considered grown-ups, even when they seemed to be acting sensible, under current federal law. So a foolish white boy could get himself in a whole lot of trouble acting silly with silly little Comanche gals who might or might not be listed as government wards by the B.I.A.

He didn't ask Tupombi if she was as they strode up the dusty street together. He knew some breeds were while others were not. Just as he knew the only thing that lied worse than a man with a hard-on was a woman feeling "unfulfilled." That was what gals said they were when they were feeling horny, "unfulfilled."

The Concord with its mule team had naturally swung around to the back by the time Longarm and Tupombi joined the new arrivals in the main waiting room, along with Shoshoni Sam and the manager.

The manager said he'd just come from the kitchen and that supper would soon be ready, provided everyone there called scrambled eggs and fried venison a supper. So it was just as well the coach had come up the delta carrying plenty of mail and only four passengers, all male and two of them Mormons who meant to sup with kith or kin in town.

The jehu, a grizzled peg-leg who'd been driving the same route a good spell, warned the two Saints not to hurry, saying, "If we're running late we're running late. I don't meant to leave here till well after daybreak in the morrow, after hearing Mister Lo is off the reserve this fall again!"

He wasn't the only one there staring sort of pensively at the obvious Indian Longarm had come in with. So Longarm quietly told the jehu, "She's with me and other mild-mannered folks here. Before you tell us about wild Indians, might you know anything of a party of white government men headed this way from Ogden for way longer than it should have taken 'em to crawl on their hands and knees?"

The somewhat younger shotgun man volunteered, "That's who warned us about the Indians. We met up with 'em this very afternoon, forted up beside the trail where it fords Club Creek."

Longarm consulted his mental map, located the dumb place they'd picked, and decided, "Indians or no Indians, they could have made it in to town by now from that close!"

The jehu nodded and said, "We just did. Allowing for my swell driving, they could be coming in anytime now. Only they won't be. They're scared. I mean, there must be over a dozen of the timid souls, with plenty of shooting irons and no women or children along. But they told us they mean to stay put there for the night, the yellow-bellied greenhorns."

His shotgun man hesitated, then decided, "Fair is fair and their scouts *did* tell 'em to stay put whilst they rode on ahead."

One of the two remaining passengers volunteered, "It was the two more experienced scouts they'd hired in Ogden who spotted Shoshoni sign and ordered the party to fort up while they scouted ahead. None of us saw any Shoshoni. On the other hand we were moving as fast as spit skips across a hot stove."

"The Shoshoni ain't supposed to be on the warpath this autumn," Longarm said. "Those gents from the B.I.A. and Land Use were sent all the way out here to *treat* with the local Shoshoni bands. So why in blue blazes would they be trying avoid meeting up with any?"

The jehu shrugged and growled, "Don't look at us. Blacky here just told you none of us saw any Shoshoni!"

The passenger called Blacky, an obvious mining man who seemed to know his way around these parts, explained, "It was the greenhorns' scouts, the missing ones, who said the Indians were acting sort of spooky. They must have known what they were talking about, whatever it was they'd spotted, for they've been missing entire ever since they had their dudes fort up and rode off!"

The manager's drab Lulu came in to tell them, or warn them, it was supper time. So they all filed in to the dining room. Tupombi went on back to the kitchen to help the other two women without having to be asked. Longarm had already noticed she was pretty and smelled as clean as most gals who rode astride in deerskin. It was a joy to see she had some manners as well.

After that the meal was rough and ready, with the fancy perked coffee making up for the overdone eggs and greasy venison. Sort of. One almost had to admire a cook who could fuck up eggs and ruin well-hung venison. It showed a sincere ambition to stay out of kitchens as often as possible.

The three gals joined in once all the menfolk had been served. Longarm wasn't surprised, or displeased, to see

Tupombi pull her chair up to his table. He'd picked that table with a view to jawing some more with the jehu and shotgun man. They seemed to want to talk more about some gals they knew up at the Montana end of their run, until Tupombi joined them and they had to talk cleaner. So they all about agreed those missing scouts could have simply gotten lost after bragging they knew more than they really did about these parts. At that point a Mormon kid in a straw hat and bib overalls came in to ask which one of them might be Deputy Long.

When Longarm pled guilty the kid came over to hand him a sheaf of neatly handwritten papers, saying he worked for Bishop Reynolds and that these papers had to be signed before they went into the county records.

Longarm told the kid to sit a spell while he read what he and Miss Tupombi were supposed to sign. When the shotgun man asked the young Saint if he'd like some coffee, the kid turned the jest back on him by saying he'd rather have a snort of Napoleon brandy, if they had any. They then decided to talk to him as they might to any good old boy.

Longarm paid little attention, at first, while he scanned the fairly accurate transcript of his early conversation with Bishop Reynolds. The church elder and county deputy had a sharp ear and a good memory for what he heard. Longarm signed and passed the papers and his indelible pencil on to Tupombi, warning her to read the page she was supposed to sign before she did so. Just then he heard something about Indians across the table.

He swung around and asked the Mormon kid to repeat that last part about smoke talk. So the Mormon kid said, "Jim Colgan, riding for the Circle Bar, saw it. They're gentiles but otherwise decent enough. Jim rode in special to warn anyone who hadn't noticed. Seems the Shoshoni have been sending smoke signals from the hogbacks over to the east. You can see way out across the range and over miles of the Overland Trail from any of them high hogbacks, you know."

The jehu and his shotgun man had heard all that the first time. After the kid had repeated it for Longarm the jehu shrugged and said, "Well, they can't be sending smoke signals about us, and them government men are down the other way, by Club Creek."

Longarm muttered grimly, "Another party headed north just a few hours ago. Do any of you gents know another professional guide who, answers to Rhinegold? Ira Rhinegold, I think he said his name was."

Nobody there had ever heard of Dame Flora's guide, let alone Dame Flora and those other Scotch pilgrims. The shotgun man opined, "Anyone else out yonder with eyes in his head would have seen as much smoke rising as that cowhand Colgan."

Longarm nodded grimly and said, "I know. So where are they, if that smoke talk inspired that cowhand to head back this way?"

The shotgun man suggested, "Same place them two missing scouts from that other party wound up?"

Longarm sighed. "I sure hope none of 'em wound up where white folks have been known to wind up during a real rising. Two of the folks we're jawing about are women, and nobody deserves to wind up the way I've found more than one poor soul, sort of scattered out on the range."

Tupombi handed the signed papers back, smiling sort of uncertainly, as she murmured, "It's not our fault. After Taiowa told Kokyangwuti to fashion us real people, she asked Sotuknang to give us our share of air, water, and earth. But he gave us hunting grounds surrounded on all sides by strangers, strangers who always wanted to fight us!"

Longarm dryly muttered, "Or vice versa. Are you trying to tell us you Comanche and your Shoshoni cousins haven't killed more strangers, red or white, than all the other nations combined?"

She smiled sweetly and replied, "That's true, and I counted coup on my mother's people. Our young men are fierce as

106

Real Bear and sly as Old Man Coyote and, as you just said, the Shoshoni are Ho too!"

Longarm got to his feet, saying, "Excuse me, folks. I got to get it on up the trail and see about some Scotch folk now."

But as he headed out the archway, slipping his frock coat back on over his gun rig, Tupombi tagged along, demanding, "Where do you think you are going, to do what, at this hour? Hear me, Custis, my Shoshoni cousins may not be after anyone at all. Sometimes smoke talk is no more than idle gossip."

He told her, "First I'm going up to fetch my McClellan and Winchester. Then I reckon I'll ride out on that roan, tired as it may be. For the paint would be too easy to spot at a distance in the moonlight."

She followed him up the stairs, protesting, "Don't be such a dumb *honaheyheya*! My Shoshoni cousins are not supposed to be on the warpath. If they are not, there is nothing to worry about. If they are, those other Taibo are already dead, and how are they supposed to answer you if you ride in circles after them in the dark?"

"They could be forted up," Longarm answered, opening the door of his hired room.

She followed him in, insisting, "In that case they are already safer for the night than you would be, playing *nanipka* in the dark with roving war parties, like a willful child, until they catch you and you're it. My mother's people don't play hide and seek by your rules, and forget that bullshit you've heard about Indians not wanting to fight in the dark!"

He chuckled and said, "I told you before I'd scouted for the army in my misspent youth. The damn fool who put that nonsense in an early guidebook must have gotten a heap of greenhorns killed by this time. I remember this shavetail fresh out of the Point who didn't think he needed to post night pickets along the Bozeman Trail during Red Cloud's War and . . . Never mind. I got to see what I can do for them Scotch folk, and meanwhile, I want you to stay here and keep an eye on my other pony for me."

She stamped a softly shod little foot and said she'd do no such thing. "Just let me get my own few things from my own room down the hall and you'll be mighty glad I came along when and if I have to talk someone out of lifting the hair off your thick head!"

He started to argue. But she seemed as determined and her words made some sense. Lewis and Clark had been mighty glad they'd had a fluent Ho-speaker along that time they'd run into the Shoshoni band of their pretty young guide, Sacajawea. With any luck at all now the Indians were still sparring for position, whatever might be bothering them.

He asked about that as he followed the pretty breed down the hall. She said it made no sense to her either if those government gents were really dealing in good faith with as smart an old cuss as Chief Pocatello. He followed her into her own room, and realized he might have made a tactical error when Tupombi slammed the door shut and turned and grabbed for him in the sudden darkness.

He suspected she'd played this sort of *nanipka* in the dark in the past, judging from her aim as she took advantage of the load he was packing to kiss him, French, and grope him, dirty, at the same time.

He let go of his saddle to grab her back, if only in self-defense, as she demurely hoisted her fringed deerskin skirts to run a naked thigh between his legs when they wound up against the securely shut door. He savored her sweet kissing a spell, being only human, but warned her as they came up for air, "I'd sure like to, Miss Tupombi. I want you so bad right now I can taste it. But there's a time and a place for everything, and we'd never forgive ourselves if we found out Dame Flora and her party were being tortured to death all the time we were enjoying one another!"

She hadn't been wearing anything at all under that red deerskin, and began to rub her fuzzy little self against the bulging front of his tweed pants as she clung tightly to him, husking,

"Speak for yourself. I'm not going to let them torture you, Custis. Not if I have to shame myself all the way with you right here and now!"

He was feeling mighty ashamed of the way his old organ-grinder was rising to the occasion despite his determination to behave in a more responsible manner. He caught himself wondering whether it would matter if they tore off just a quick one to sort of settle their nerves before they rode out to see if Dame Flora and her party needed help. Then he gently but firmly stiff-armed Tupombi away, growling, "Hold the thought, and once we know what's up out yonder I promise I'll get it up for you some more."

When she tried to press close again his voice got harder, saying, "I mean it, honey. I'm a lawman first and a ladies' man when it don't stand betwixt me and my duty. So stand aside and let me be on my damned way with or without your help, hear?"

Before she could answer they both stiffened in each other's arms at the roar of at least two revolvers, big ones, blasting the shit out of something, or somebody, close!

Longarm shoved the little breed gal so hard she wound up flat on her bed covers across the room. He hadn't meant to shove her that hard but damn it, she'd been in the way of his cross-draw as he'd spun and grabbed the knob with his other fist.

He had his .44–40 out as he slid out into the hallway from a direction that other cuss down the way must not have expected. The buckskin-clad stranger gasped in wide-eyed terror as he turned from the smoke-filled doorway of Longarm's original room, two smoking .45–55 Schofields in hand, as Longarm told him conversationally, "Drop them guns and grab some rafters *now!*"

The mysterious stranger hesitated. So Longarm fired thrice, dead center between those fucking gun muzzles trained his way, and that, of course, inspired the unfortunate who'd just shot up his room to stagger back, bounce off a stucco wall, and thud wetly to the floorboards faceup, atop the nastier exit wounds of Longarm's rapid fire through his rib cage.

Longarm stayed where he was, reloading, as Tupombi joined him by her doorway while others called up the stairs at them. Longarm called back, "Somebody best fetch Bishop Reynolds some more. I suspect I just got the one who got away this afternoon."

Moving in through the clearing smoke with his own gun loaded six-in-the-wheel, Longarm spotted one of the other man's bigger thumb-busters on the floor between baseboard and bloody buckskin. The stoutly framed army-issue revolver had been rechambered for those more lethal rounds and fitted with tailored grips, likely Mex, carved from mussel shell or maybe real mother-of-pearl. So Longarm muttered, "Howdy, Pearly. Now all we got to figure out is the true identity of Pappy, after which we might be able to figure out why killing me was so important to you determined rascals."

Tupombi pointed through the clearing smoke at some goose down floating out the door of Longarm's room. He nodded and said, "Yep, it was my own poor feather bed he just shot the liver and lights out of, the poor bastard."

He couldn't resist adding, with a lopsided grin, "Ain't you glad you waited till we was in your room before you tried to get us both into such a ridiculous position?"

Chapter 9

The gunplay had naturally been heard all over a town as modest as that one, and one advantage of small-town crowds for a lawman was the simple fact that most everyone in such a crowd knew most everyone else in town. So it didn't take long to establish Pearly as a total stranger to those parts as well.

This time Bishop Reynolds showed up with his temporal boss, a High Sheriff Alcott who didn't rank as high in church affairs but still seemed a Saint it wasn't safe to offer a cheroot to. So Longarm didn't, and when he said he had to ride on after those Scotch folk as soon as possible, the stern old High Sheriff told him it wasn't possible, but that he'd send a posse comitatus out to bring Dame Flora and her party back, dead or alive.

Meanwhile, having shot two men within twenty-four hours in or about Zion County, Descret, they thought the least a gentile stranger who claimed to be a lawman could do would be to explain some of this infernal gunplay at a formal sit-down with the county coroner, who was off somewhere hunting strays at the moment. It didn't really cheer Longarm all that much to learn they'd elected a gentile stockman with some knowledge of veterinary medicine as their county coroner.

But after some consideration Longarm decided it might be best if he went along with the local lawmen, who knew the

111

local lay of the land way better than he did.

It stood to reason a posse of riders familiar with the rugged range this side of Fort Hall would be able to search it at least as thoroughly, in far safer numbers. And besides, he'd still been sent all this way to ride herd on those other dudes, bogged down or forted up, whichever, in the other direction entirely.

The manager allowed they'd be proud to overnight him some more, and rustled him up another room, a couple of doors closer to the one Tupombi and his possibles were in. He didn't say so as Lulu led him up there after things had simmered down and then left him unmolested to go back down and molest the manager some more.

Longarm lit a sneaky cheroot from the candlestick Lulu had left him and smoked it down, reclined across the unwounded feather bed with the window sash flung wide. Then, figuring the others had bedded down for a spell, he got back up and slipped out into the mighty dark hallway without that lit candlestick. For he knew where he was headed and it was nobody else's beeswax.

Tupombi opened up, although just a candlelit slit, without yelling through the door he'd tapped on discreetly. He could still see she didn't go to bed in deerskins. But she was standing sideways lest he spy anything important as she braced her bare hip against that damned door, murmuring, "Heavens, I was almost asleep and what are you doing at my door at this hour, Custis?"

He said, "Rapping on it, of course. Ain't you fixing to invite a man in for just a minute?"

It was tough to read her eyes with all the light coming from behind her bare ass like that. So when she fluttered her lashes and demanded to know what sort of a girl he thought she was, he decided to take her at her word. He didn't know any Indian words for "prick-teaser," although that game was hardly confined to the gals of his own persuasion.

He said, "I ain't out to trifle with any wards of the government, Miss Tupombi. I only need some stuff from my saddlebags, and as you'd likely notice if you'd be kind enough to glance down, my old McClellan should be somewhere on your floorboards betwixt the doorjamb and the baseboard."

She said, "Oh," in an oddly pouting way. Then she told him to hold on just a moment, and shut the door in his face. Before he could get sore, however, she opened it again wider, and he saw she'd wrapped a towel around her tawny young charms. Indians didn't worry as much as Queen Victoria about bare shoulders and thighs.

He stepped inside with a tick of his hat brim and a nod of his thanks to simply bend over and pick up the saddle with other gear lashed to it. He'd been right about where it had landed amid the earlier confusion. As he straightened back up with the McClellan braced on one hip the pretty little breed softly murmured, "You used to call me honey, and I told you I was educated white, and I never applied to the B.I.A. for an allotment number when I went back to my mother in my teens."

To which he could only reply, with a wistful smile, "I've been known to call a lady all sorts of sweet things whilst we kissed a mite sassy, Miss Tupombi. But seeing we seem to have had us some second thoughts, I'll just tote this saddle and the rest of my awkward self out of your cooled-down presence, hear?"

He meant it. Women could tell, and it only counted when men meant it. So she somehow managed to bar the whole way out with her pretty little self as she sort of sobbed, "Don't speak to me so coldly. I was only trying to keep you from riding out in the dark to certain death. I wasn't trying to tease you, Custis. But now that we don't have to worry about that . . ."

"Nothing's certain but death and taxes," he said, adding, "If you're rich enough you don't even have to pay the taxes. But I get your general drift, and I'm glad you were so anxious to save my life for me, ma'am. It was an experience I'll never forget."

She didn't move her towel-wrapped hips from the door latch. He hesitated an awkward moment and softly asked, "Can I go, now, ma'am?"

113

She let go of the towel. As it limply peeled away from her slender but curvacious tawny torso in the soft romantic candlelight he was too thunderstruck to say anything. So it was she who asked, with a knowing expression, whether he really wanted to go.

As she'd doubtless suspected he might, Longarm let go of his dumb old saddle, skimmed his Stetson across to the chest of drawers, and hauled the naked lady in for an even friendlier kiss than that last time. But as they came up for air, with her groping at his buttons, she pleaded with him not to tease her anymore. So he swept her up in his arms, carried her over to her bed, and was in her, deep, with both pillows under her bounding buttocks, before he'd bothered with all his own duds.

She found it as amusing to help him undress without taking it out or even slowing down, once they had those infernal boots off. By that time they'd both come, Tupombi more than once, and so it was a calmer and more relaxed Longarm who settled in for a long bareback lope across clean sheets and a goose-down mattress. He had to chuckle as he thought back to his anthropology experiments with old Sandy Henderson back at that museum. For just as he'd told that curious redhead, gals used to screwing in a tipi screwed much the same as everyone else in a feather bed.

The only sign Tupombi gave of holding with some Indian notions was when she locked her bare ankles around the nape of his neck, dug her nails into his writhing behind, and sobbed, *"Hai-hai-yee! Ta soon da hipey!"* which hardly needed much translation because he was coming at the same time.

After that they put her candle out and shared a smoke in the cool darkness as they let their overheated flesh rest up and dry a bit. She smoked Indian-style, taking longer, deeper drags and trying to swallow it for keeps. He knew that in most dialects the Indian verbs for smoke and drink were the same. He liked his own way of smoking better, and it wasn't as if they were having some formal tobacco ceremony then and there.

114

He asked about that as he snuggled her bare flesh against his own. She said Pocatello and his Shoshoni-Bannock sub-chiefs would likely pass the calumet around with those gents from back East, if ever they wound up anywhere near Fort Hall. He was amused when she added, "My mother's people know your people don't feel a treaty has any *puha* unless everyone smokes from the same calumet. Most of our *powamu* keep a pretty calumet on hand for such occasions."

He laughed, took a drag on his less-impressive cheroot, and asked how Ho-speakers made peace with other Indians if a peace pipe wasn't all that important.

She explained, "Oh, we Ho you call Comanche make the same promises, with the same ceremonies, to everyone we don't want to fight with at the moment. It's usually a good idea to make peace with an enemy who has the advantage. It gives you the chance to recover and get back at the *heyheyas* when *you* have the advantage."

He passed her the smoke, muttering, "You sound like our General Phil Sheridan. He's always held peace treaties with warrior clans to be a waste of paper and tobacco too. So how might a Ho-speaker really make peace, to fight no more forever, like Chief Joseph agreed that time?"

She didn't reply until she burped a tiny puff back up. Then she passed the cheroot back to him, saying, "Heinmot Tooyalket, the one you call Joseph, was not Ho and never made any peace with anybody of his own free will. He fought you until he had been beaten, beaten, and had no more *puha*."

Longarm frowned uncertainly up at the dark ceiling as he mused, half to himself, "Pocatello and his young men have been mauled a time or two, but they've never been whipped to a frazzle and found themselves pinned down so many miles from home. So let me put it another way. How might a Ho-speaking chief who still leads a heap of young men, in his own country, make a lasting peace with that commission I've been sent to back, if only I ever meet up with the sons of bitches?"

115

She answered simply, "I don't know. My mother's people don't make peace with anyone for long unless they really like them. A Ho goes by what he or she feels inside, not by what has been said with tobacco smoke or ink."

"Then those Shoshoni acting odd over to the foothills could be feeling something mean inside?"

"Of course. That's why I'm going to fuck you all night and keep them from killing you. Get rid of that silly cheroot and let me show you how *I* feel inside."

Chapter 10

Come morning, the Overland manager had rustled up some local farm kids to replace his missing kitchen and dining-room staff. He said he didn't care if old Pete Robbins ever showed up again or not. He was sore as hell at the moonshining bastard for leaving them in such a fix and he'd said as much, in writing, to his district supervisor up Montana way.

That Montana-bound coach had already left, along with his letter, by the time Longarm and Tupombi heard about it at breakfast. The two of them had risen sort of late that morning, and Shoshoni Sam seemed a mite annoyed about that when he finally caught up with them at their corner table, as they inhaled bacon, eggs, and plenty of the strong black coffee the new cooks had brewed out in the kitchen despite the Book of Mormon.

Shoshoni Sam said he and Madame Marvella had been up for hours, and that those riders had reported back after finding neither the Scotch folk nor any Indians who might have been after them, so when were they fixing to ride out after Sacajawea some more?

Tupombi glanced shyly at Longarm, who said, "Don't look at me. I can't ride on before I've had a few words with the local coroner, and even then, I'd best wait here for those other federal men."

Tupombi said it sounded safer if they all waited there for that far bigger government party. She sounded sincere, even to Longarm, as she explained, "They should have broken camp to the south by now, if they haven't gotten into a fight with anyone. If they have gotten into a fight, and haven't been able to break out, I don't think I want to leave town with only two or even three people."

Shoshoni Sam sighed and said, "You sound as bad as Madame Marvella. She's been pestering me to turn back ever since she heard about them smoke signals."

Longarm meant it when he quietly suggested, "You could do way worse than listen to the lady, Sam. The road ahead keeps getting rougher, with or without Indian trouble. I should have told you sooner that Fort Hall's just a dinky agency with few facilities for travelers."

"We can't turn back before we find out whether Sacajawea is still alive and willing to join up with us!" the older man shouted.

Longarm shrugged and said, "Seems to me she'd have joined up with someone, or at least written a book by now, if she felt so inclined and that ain't her buried up to Fort Union. I mean, all sorts of folks who've been west of the Big Muddy more than a week have written a heap of books and given heaps of lectures, dressed in snow-white beaded buckskins, whilst the one and original Sacajawea *did* see way more of the West, in its Shining Times, and they say she learned how to read and write, in English, French, and Lord knows how many Indian dialects."

He reached for an after-breakfast smoke, the new Mormon help being accommodating, as he elaborated. "We're talking about a woman who had access to President Thomas Jefferson in the flesh, and we know he was mighty interested in Indian matters. So how come Sacajawea was never asked to jot down just a simple dictionary of the half-dozen Indian lingos Lewis and Clark agreed she was fluent in?"

Shoshoni Sam said he didn't know. Tupombi quietly suggested, "Maybe she didn't want to. It's bad *puha* to even repeat some words in my mother's language. It couldn't be a good idea to freeze them forever, always, on paper."

Shoshoni Sam said that sounded like a mighty poor way to preserve any lingo. Longarm said, "I think I can explain. We ain't the only ones who think some words have more medicine than others."

The showman demanded an example. So Longarm looked away from the lady in their presence as he softly suggested, "You might try substituting shit for manure, in mixed company, if you'd like to see how some words hit harder than others meaning the same thing. Miss Tupombi here can correct me if I'm wrong, but I've also been told it's bad medicine to say anything about anyone you ever knew who might be dead."

Tupombi nodded soberly and said, "*Ayee,* that is true. I can remember my poor mother as Laughing Dancer, because that was how we said her name in Taibo. But all four of her ghosts would be upset with me if I ever repeated her name in Ho!"

Longarm added, "Meaning there's a tendency to change such words as laughing or dancing to, say, amused or prancing. A pal of mine who studies Indians thinks they started out with no more than two or three distinct lingos. The hundreds recorded so far are the combined results of changing words on purpose and, like we just heard, not wanting to pin anything down on paper for keeps."

Tupombi nodded and said, "The Shoshoni ahead used to speak just the same as my mother's people. We can still understand one another clearly. But in the time since our bands first parted we've begun to sound a little different. I find it even harder to understand a Paiute, and I'm not sure the Chihuahua are real people at all."

Longarm assured her Chihuahua didn't think much of Comanche, and turned back to Shoshoni Sam to say, "There you go. Even if you did find an old lady who remembered Lewis and Clark, she'd likely refuse to say their names out loud and then where would you be?"

They were still arguing about it when Bishop Reynolds came in with a jovial-looking gentile in batwing chaps and a hat almost as floppy, whom he introduced as Greg Lukas, their county coroner when he wasn't raising beef or doctoring sick ponies. So Longarm took his leave of Tupombi and Shoshoni Sam to drift over by the town dump, where they were fixing to plant the second stranger Longarm had shot it out with so recently.

As the three of them walked the short distance Bishop Reynolds told Longarm he'd explained the gunplay as best he knew how. When Longarm commenced to give his own version, the coroner cut in with an easygoing, "I heard. Stands to reason a man has every right to gun a son of a bitch who's just shot the stuffings outten his goose-down mattress, even when he ain't a federal lawman."

When Longarm said he was glad to see they'd taken him at his word, Lukas chuckled dryly and said, "Oh, I reckon we had us some solid evidence as well. The bullets we dug outten your hired bedstead were all .45 caliber, as were the chambers of his two pearl-handled six-guns. Both his guns were empty when you caught up with him, by the way. But that's all right. You couldn't have known, and the slugs you put through him were all .44. We dug 'em out of the plaster earlier. So everything you told Deputy Reynolds here was in total agreement with the material evidence. I don't suppose you've figured out why either of 'em might have been after you?"

Longarm shook his head and truthfully replied, "I can't figure out who either of 'em could have *been*. Nobody from these parts has been able to identify either and I've searched my brain, more than once, for any wanted outlaws who describe at all the same."

Lukas indicated a path between two monstrous piles of rusting tin cans as he said, "We've taken photographs of both of 'em, for future reference. I'd still like you to have a last peek, by broad day, at the one you gunned last night in such murky light."

Longarm agreed that made sense. As the three of them came out the far side of the pass through the range of rusty cans, Longarm saw a couple of other gents, dressed cow, on their feet by a pile of fresh dirt near the center of a weed-grown and trash-littered quarter acre. As they drew nearer he spied two feet, wearing no more than wool socks. The poor cuss he'd shot lay in just those socks, his pants, and his bloodstained shirt on the far side of the pile. The shallow grave they'd dug for him lay just beyond. Lukas called out, cheerfully, "Just hold the thought, boys. This lawman who kilt the rascal would like a last look at the same."

The grave-diggers stepped back. Longarm strode closer, paused, and stared soberly down at the Mona Lisa smile of a total stranger. He already knew the one called Pearly had been packing no identification at all, even fake. He looked to have been around twenty-five, or a tad older than the one he'd called Kid. When Longarm asked about that one, Lukas pointed with his chin at a slightly mounded bare patch, saying, "Already feeding the worms. They planted him late yesterday the way you arranged. He was already turning funny colors, I'm told, and the county can't afford embalming for drifters nobody cares about."

Longarm gazed about the disturbed and sort of disturbing plot as he couldn't help noting, "Bishop Reynolds here already told me that. I see you don't bother marking the graves neither?"

Lukas shrugged. "Why should we? We got a fair idea where we've planted someone recently, and nobody never comes to put no flowers on the graves. We got us regular Mormon and gentile churchyards here in Zion, Deputy Long. Nobody anyone ever gave a shit about winds up here in Potter's Field."

Longarm nodded. "Well, I can't say I was all too fond of this poor bastard, whoever he might have been. I sure would like photo prints of both of 'em before I leave, but as of right now, your guess is as good as mine."

Lukas nodded and one of his hired hands nudged the body with a boot heel to roll it, stiff as a plank, into its grave. It landed facedown. Longarm was just as glad when they commenced to kick and then scoop dirt in on top of the cadaver they were planting without even a muslin shroud. It helped some to reflect on how they'd have left *him* for the carrion crows had things turned out the way they'd planned the day before.

Walking back to town with the coroner and the others, Longarm casually asked just how many unmarked graves they could be talking about back yonder. Lukas thought before he answered. "Two dozen tops. Some before my time. You don't get many unclaimed dead folks in an out-of-the-way town like this, even though it is the county seat."

Bishop Reynolds nodded. "We take care of our own. Overland takes care of the few who die aboard its coaches on their way to or from the gold fields."

There was barely time enough for the locals to recall half the six or eight vagrants buried back yonder since Lukas had taken over as coroner a couple of summers back. Then one of the Mormon townsmen met them on the far side of the trash piles to tell old Bishop Reynolds a bunch of gentile riders were coming in from the south, lathered and still riding hard.

Longarm figured, and everyone agreed, it sounded like that government party. As they spied a stationary column of dust down the road ahead Lukas observed, "Looks as if they've reined in at the Overland stop."

Longarm said, "I noticed. They come all this way to treat with Indians and it seems the Indians have scared 'em shitless. I got to find out why."

That was easier said than done, once they joined the confusion all around the Overland stop. A dozen sweaty and dusty riders could run in heaps of circles, and their two dozen ponies and six or eight pack mules weren't making much more sense as they argued about who got watered first.

Once he'd established the boss men were already inside, Longarm tracked them down in the smoke-filled dining room, with Reynolds and Lukas following him. Those ranch hands and grave-diggers who worked for Lukas both ways went around to the back to lend their know-how with stock to some poor souls who didn't seem to have the knack.

Longarm and his own companions found a portly red-faced cuss of, say, fifty gulping coffee and puffing cigar smoke across that same corner table at a slightly older and far skinnier cuss with a hatchet face and superior brand of cigar. Longarm couldn't have afforded to smoke with either of them on a regular basis, but even so they were both dressed less refined, in sort of dusty Davy Crockett outfits. Longarm was too polite to ask why, or to point out Davy Crockett had been dressed more like a white man when he'd headed out to Texas as a grown-up. Indians and white folks who had to live like Indians wore buckskin because they had nothing better. Had machine-woven textiles not felt better against human skin wet or dry, there'd have been no point in inventing half as many textile machines. But you'd never guess that from Currier and Ives prints or half the covers of the current Wild West magazines, and so even old Bill Cody seemed to think he had to gussy up like a Cheyenne squaw lest someone accuse him of being just off the boat.

As Longarm introduced himself and his local associates to the apparent mountain men of an earlier era, the fat one owned up to being a congressman called Granger, serving on some congressional committee, while the skinny one was a Senator Rumford, the nominal head of the outfit. Granger, who seemed most likely to kiss babies and chew the fat, said they'd been worried sick about Longarm long before they'd lost those other two Indian experts.

When Longarm smiled uncertainly and allowed he'd been told they had at least one real Indian as well as Indian experts along, the more morose Senator Rumford explained, "The B.I.A. loaned us a couple of Paiute, in the beginning. They quit soon after we told them they might meet Bannock up at Fort Hall."

Longarm nodded. "They do say Bannock used to ride down

123

Paiute just for practice. Lord knows few wandering diggers have a thing worth taking, save for their scalps. But I reckon us cruel white folks ain't the only ones who bully the weak without all that much reason, the way dogs chase cats. You say you're missing some white scouts as well?"

Senator Rumford made a wry face and replied, "We're still working on whether they deserted or whether Indians got them. They had us dig in, down the other side of Club Creek, while they scouted on ahead."

"That's the last we ever saw of them," the portly Granger said, waving his claro like a smoldering baton. "It was over forty-eight hours ago and we knew we were within running distance of this safer settlement. Pearly and The Kid said they'd seen something *else* ahead, bless their cautious hearts, and—"

"Hold her right there!" Longarm thundered as Bishop Reynolds and his country coroner exchanged startled looks. Longarm demanded, "Could we be talking about a husky cuss in his mid-twenties, sporting pearl-handled Schofields, and a younger cuss armed less dramatically?"

It was the turn of Granger and Rumford to exchange startled glances indeed as Longarm filled them in on Pearly and The Kid as soon as they'd confirmed his descriptions.

When Senator Rumford half rose from the table, ashen-faced, to accuse Longarm of having made a terrible mistake, the still-standing Longarm shook his head firmly and replied, "It was them who made the terrible mistake, Senator. They never took me for any Indian when they opened up on me in the open, and after that, I heard 'em jawing back and forth about me personally. They knew it was me, and somebody they called Pappy had sent them after me with murderous intent!"

Bishop Reynolds volunteered, "The one with the pearl-handled .45–55s was not registered here as a guest last night. Deputy Long here was. His room number would have been in the unguarded register behind the deserted desk for anyone to read at that hour."

Longarm cocked an eyebrow at the older lawman and said, "I do admire a peace officer who plays his own cards as close to his vest. Need I add it was Pearly, not me, who flung a door open and blew the liver and lights out of a bed he had every reason to expect me to be bedded down in?"

The crusty old Saint smiled thinly and replied, "You need not, and I've a fair notion which room you came out of instead. But let's stick to pure and simple gunplay."

Longarm did, and soon established, with the help of Granger and Rumford, that the reason Longarm had gotten so far ahead of the other government men had been the two scouts' constant talk of Indians, with them getting everyone else to dig in, over and over, while they scouted ahead.

"For me," Longarm decided modestly enough as soon as he'd had time to consider other options. Lest anyone there think he had too high an opinion of himself, he explained, "You gents had been told I'd be joining up with your expedition. Somebody must not have been too keen about that. By bogging you down at least every few miles, they got to scout out all around in hopes of heading me off, as they finally did in their own half-ass way."

Senator Rumford started to ask a dumb question, then proved he wasn't so dumb, despite his New England twang, by declaring, "I see it now. Anyone can *say* they're only scouting out ahead. They did take their own sweet time, time enough to scout our back trail as well as the trail ahead."

"Why ahead at all?" asked the portly Granger.

To which Longarm could only modestly reply, "They figured there was a chance I'd head you off. They figured right. At the rate you gents were moving, no offense, I could have headed you off afoot."

Senator Rumford didn't sound offended as he explained, "We felt we had to move with caution in such wild country. We're carrying a modest fortune in freshly coined silver dollars, you know."

Bishop Reynolds demanded to know who'd told them the Mormon Delta was such wild country. Longarm shut him off with a soothing smile and said, "Never mind all that. Tell us what you'd call a modest fortune in silver, Senator."

Rumford said, "Sixty thousand dollars, adding up to just under a couple of tons of specie. The damned fool Indians demanded it. They simply can't seem to grasp the concept of paper money."

Longarm whistled softly and then dryly suggested, "I ain't sure I'd put much faith in anything on paper if I was an Indian with sixty thousand dollars' worth of anything to sell. I was wondering about them big old pack mules. Might I ask just what the taxpayers are out to buy with that much solid silver?"

Granger volunteered, "At least four hundred thousand acres the Shoshoni-Bannock bands don't really need, this side of the Snake River."

Senator Rumford confirmed both Washington and Salt Lake felt the land in question would be much improved by white settlers because the otherwise-fertile soil needed irrigation works to bring it up to its full potential.

When Granger added something about Indians not understanding a thing about agriculture, Longarm managed not to mention those vast irrigation projects Indians had come up with down to the southwest before Columbus had been a gleam in his daddy's eye. He said instead, "That many acres of pure-ass desert would be a bargain at double your offer, no offense. So them Shoshoni must want that silver awesomely bad!"

He reached for one of his own smokes in self-defense, muttering half to himself, "So how come the Shoshoni have been acting so spooky of late?"

When Granger suggested their treacherous scouts, for whatever reason, could have been just making up some Indian trouble, it was Bishop Reynolds's turn to declare, "Some Indians have been sending up smoke signals to the north, and Shoshoni are about all the Indians we get in these parts."

Lukas nodded and said, "Bannock seldom ride this far south since Buffalo Horn got his fool self shot acting sassy that time. Some of my riders have reported smoke talk over to the foothills too. That's how come I been out rounding up my herd the last few days."

Longarm asked the stockman how many head he might be missing. The Easterners couldn't see why until Lukas allowed he didn't seem to be missing enough to matter, adding, "They can't be raiding us for livestock, after all. Lord only knows what they're *really* talking over with all that infernal smoke!"

Longarm frowned uncertainly and ventured, "It could be no more than us. Whether we were coming or not, I mean. If old Pocatello demanded two tons of silver for anything, he surely expects to see it before the first real snowfall."

Granger said with a pout that neither he nor the stock would be ready to push on for at least a spell. Then two more men from their outfit came in, followed by Shoshoni Sam, Madame Marvella, and a mighty innocent-looking Tupombi. So seeing he was going to have to start all over again, Longarm suggested they haul over an extra table and more chairs. Bishop Reynolds got out of helping by heading out to the kitchen to demand some damned service.

The two new government men were an Indian agent and a head mule teamster with at least one Indian grandparent, both loaned by the B.I.A. Tim McBride, the whiter of the two, allowed he'd been deputy agent at the White River Agency in Colorado before the Utes there had been pushed across the Green River into less civilized range. Duke Pearson, the breed, said he'd been allowed to go on driving mules trains most anywhere because his grandmother's Ute band had been smart enough to steer clear of the Meeker Massacre and such. Neither B.I.A. man had any fringes or beadwork on or about their persons. They were both dressed for comfort on the trail in sort of uncertain autumn weather. Either one of them could have passed for a hand employed by Lukas digging graves or punching cows.

By the time they had all of that straightened out they'd all found seats at the two shoved-together tables. By the time a weary Longarm had repeated a tale he was commencing to find tedious, the Mormon kids from the kitchen had everyone there but the bishop sipping coffee and nibbling marble cake. Bishop Reynolds had his cake with buttermilk.

After confirming suspicions he'd already had about those two so-called scouts, Tim McBride opined, "They were slowing us down deliberate, more than they really needed to if all they had in mind was dry-gulching Deputy Long here."

Before anyone could answer, McBride brightened and asked, "Say, might you be the Deputy Long called Longarm, the one the Utes call Saltu Ka Saltu?"

Longarm nodded modestly. Duke Pearson grinned too and said, "Well, I swan, and wait till I tell the folk back home I met up with the gent who arrested that son-of-a-bitching agent who was robbing 'em blind that time."

Then he remembered there were women present, stammered as much at Madame Marvella, and apparently apologized more handsomely to Tupombi in Ho. She tried not to let her suffering show as she coped with his Ute accent, and demurely replied in her more trilly Shoshoni-Comanche version of the same basic lingo.

McBride said Pearson had never noticed any Indian sign either on the trail from Ogden, and repeated his charges against the late Pearly and The Kid, whom he'd known by more formal names he now tended to doubt.

Longarm hauled out his notebook and stub pencil as he told the Indian agent, "There's a government telegraph up at Fort Hall. I got to wire in a progress report when we reach it any case. So I'd be obliged if you'd jot down the names and home addresses those rascals gave you when they signed on with the B.I.A."

McBride took the pencil and paper but explained, even as he was block-printing in Longarm's notebook, how Senator Rumford, not the B.I.A., had hired the two sneaks down in Ogden.

Senator Rumford told Longarm, "It was as much your fault as mine, Deputy Long. We'd been told you'd meet us there. When you didn't, and Thomas Wynn, the one called Pearly, warned us of some Indian trouble and offered to guide us through country they knew so much better . . ."

"We've established they were big fibbers," Longarm said.

Duke Pearson snorted, "Indian trouble! What Indian trouble this late in the game? I told you gents way back when that the Western Shoshoni never could hold a candle to real troublesome Indians, and that was before they were whipped, like cur dogs, by Colonel Connor from the Humboldt to the Bear way back when."

Tupombi said something that sounded mighty surly in Ho, then switched to English so that everyone there could follow her drift as she snapped, "Pat Connor was a child-molester and a disgrace to the colors of his own nation! Who did he fight at Bear River? Women and children! That's who he fought at Bear River!"

It was McBride who mildly mentioned the hundred-odd Shoshoni warriors camped near the Bear River with their dependents under Chief Sagwitch when Connor's Nevada Volunteers caught up with them.

Longarm liked Tupombi too much to mention George Clayton, Hank Beam, or Henry Smith, jumped and scalped by Sagwitch for no better reason than that the Shoshoni found them way out on the range alone. Pretty white ladies back in Denver didn't like to be reminded of all those South Cheyenne jumped at Sand Creek for no particular reason either. So he hushed them both, saying, "Bear Creek was years ago and Pocatello's band managed to stay out of it."

McBride grumbled, "Until he took the shot-up Sagwitch in and hid him from the troops until he was fit to fight another day, you mean!"

Longarm shrugged. "Whatever. Pocatello ain't done nothing like that recently, and seems to want to swap more Shoshoni land for silver. So the question before the house is why a cuss called Pappy, who has to be somebody else, seems so intent on queering your simple real estate transaction?"

Their local stockman, Lukas, suggested, "I wouldn't be so sure no Indians could be up to . . . whatever. I'll agree those jaspers Longarm had it out with were likely faking Indian trouble if you'll tell me who's been sending all them smoke signals, up the trail where neither of them dead rascals could have ever been."

Bishop Reynolds frowned thoughtfully and declared, "We don't know that. If they told the senator here they knew the country, who's to say they didn't know the country, and even some Indians, all the way up the trail?"

Longarm was about to point out how anyone with even a small band of hostiles in cahoots with them would hardly have to move in alone on a lawman alone, no matter what the lawman's reputation. But he had a better idea. So once he determined the older gents meant to rest up there until noon, and that Shoshoni Sam and the two gals meant to tag along with them, he persuaded just one of the gals to tag along with *him,* to his room upstairs.

Once she had, he was reminded once more of old Sandy, back at the museum in Denver, while he showed the tawny and more muscular Tupombi how some Taibo went at it dog-style, atop a feather mattress.

She found the novel position exciting. He made up for the workout she'd given him before breakfast by closing his eyes to picture a bigger redhead's paler rump as he thrust in and out a spell, then opened his eyes to stare fondly down at the renewed novelty of such a friendly Comanche ass.

So what with one position and another, the morning passed all too quickly, and then it was time to mount something less frisky, in this case his hired paint, as they all rode out to the north under a blazing noonday sun, the poor dumb sons of bitches.

Chapter 11

It could have felt worse, a lot worse, at other times or places that far west of the Big Muddy. Even those parts of Idaho Territory defined as true desert were *high* desert, with the thin dry air all around sucking the sweat out of you suddenly enough to give you a sort of chill whenever a cloud passed between you and the purely white afternoon sun, and that was in high summer.

This late in the year old Tanapah couldn't really get his back into his shining, even on the dusty Snake River Plains out ahead. So things just felt shirtsleevey as they followed the trail over rolling, partly timbered, but mostly grassy range, as long they kept moving and let their duds flap some. A lot of the grass was cheat closer to town, where the range had been overgrazed by old Lukas and other gentile stockmen who raised scrubbier beef more casually than your average Saint. The few cows they encountered naturally scattered at the sight of that many riders headed their way. Longarm doubted cows really knew what happened to them after they'd been cut from the herd to be cut up into handier portions. But it hardly mattered to any critter with Hispano-Moorish ancestry. For the Mexican-Texican longhorn had been bred to stay alive until its owner was damn well ready to slaughter it and running like hell from anything it didn't aim to eat or fuck was a good way for a cow to stay alive on open range.

After no more than three or four trail breaks they saw fewer cows and far more real grass, mostly buffalo, bunch, and grama, sun-dried to rib-sticking straw for grazing critters. Longarm had been told some buffalo had roamed this side of the Continental Divide in the Shining Times. There were old Indian tales of longhorn buffalo, bigger, meaner, and dumber than the regular kind. Longarm hadn't seen any this far west since he'd first come West just after the war. For some reason the pronghorns the more western tribes liked to hunt instead seemed to prefer the sagebrush country ahead, on somewhat lower and flatter ground. He figured he'd know better which kind of hunting ground old Pocatello had for sale when he saw some of it. The best land for farming wasn't always the best kind for hunting, and vice versa. But it figured to be piss-poor land for anything if the Indians were willing to let it go so cheap. Pocatello wasn't exactly a poor dumb Arawak, watching Columbus wade ashore. So it might be interesting to know whether the Shoshoni thought they or Uncle Sam was taking it up the ass.

It happened both ways. The old boys who'd sold Manhattan Island for twenty-odd dollars' worth of perfectly good trade goods hadn't been the only Indians who'd sold land they didn't happen to own to the paleface and nobody would have ever invented the term "Indian giver" if at least some Indians hadn't wanted their swaps back after they'd used up the salt or drank all the liquor in the jug. Pocatello was supposed to know how to read his own copy of the Book of Mormon, and he'd been smart enough to demand solid silver. So what was really going on, and why was that smoke rising over to his left? Those cowhands had said they'd spotted smoke talk above the far higher ground to his *right*.

Longarm had been riding point with Tim McBride, a quarter mile out ahead of the others. When McBride saw the same smoke and commenced to rein in Longarm muttered, "I see it. Don't let on *you* do just yet."

McBride kept pace with Longarm and his hired mount—since the last watering it had been the roan—and said, "I don't savvy that smoke talk at all."

Longarm said, "Neither do I. We're not supposed to. It ain't a regular code, like Morse. Different series of puffs mean whatever the puffer and puffee agreed on earlier. But for openers I'd say someone over to our west is telling someone else to our east about where we are, how many we are, mayhaps even *who* we are."

The Indian agent snorted and said, "That part ain't what I don't savvy. What I don't savvy is why they seem to be scouting us from low ground and signaling our whereabouts to somebody else on *high* ground!"

Longarm nodded. "I follow your drift, and for once the B.I.A. seems to have hired a white man with brains, no offense. I doubt they could be signaling anyone who already has a better view of us from those hills to our east. How do you cotton to the notion of them signaling *ahead,* say to someone just as low-down, over the horizon to our north?"

McBride agreed that made more sense, and asked what they ought to do next. So Longarm suggested, "What if you was to just keep following this same beaten path, at the same pace, with no shift in the dust column keeping pace behind us, whilst I sort of eased my way out around that smoke talk to jump 'em from behind and have a little talk with 'em?"

McBride demanded, "How? I'm pretty sure they must be on that one lone swell rising a few dozen feet above the others all about."

When Longarm agreed he had the same location in mind McBride pointed out, "They'll surely see you peeling away from the party and be long gone before you can get within miles of 'em!"

Longarm said, "We're already within miles of 'em. I make it no more than two miles out, unless they're on another swell entirely, in which case they can't see us at all, so what are we arguing about?"

McBride laughed dryly and said, "Well, you might be able to drop out as we're crossing the next draw, if it's deep enough. But they'll still spot you again the moment you ride close enough to matter."

Longarm said, "I know. That's why I mean to dismount in the first deep draw we come to, tether this pony smack by the trail, and sort of pussy-foot out and around. I wear these low-heel boots with a certain amount of pussy-footing in mind."

They heard faster hoofbeats overtaking them. As they glanced back they saw Senator Rumford and Shoshoni Sam coming fast with worried expressions. Longarm called back, "Don't point out any smoke talk to us, gents. We were just talking about 'em. Someone could be out to spook us. So don't act spooked and farther along, as the old song says, we'll know more about it."

As the two other riders joined them Longarm added he was glad they had, explaining, "Human eyes, like crow birds, only count as high as three for certain without actually counting. That's how come we say three or four. When we dip below the line of sight from yonder whatever, I'll drop out, you three will just ride on naturally, and they might not notice. It's an old crow-hunting trick. You've all no doubt hunted crows as kids by having four or five old boys go into some cover near a roost, having all but one come back out, and giving that one old boy the chance to blast the wise-ass birds when they decide it's safe to flutter down and roost some more?"

He wasn't too surprised to learn the crusty New Englander knew more about hunting crows than Shoshoni Sam. The four of them rode on another few furlongs. Then, where the trail swung down through an alder-choked draw, Longarm announced that had to be the place and reined in to haul out his Winchester and dismount while the others just kept going.

He tethered the roan to a handy alder, gave it an assuring pat, and said, "I know you'd like cottonwood leaves better, if these were only cottonwoods in leaf instead of bare-ass alders. But I reckon we all got to take

134

the luck of the draw from time to time."

Then he was moving west through other bare alders along the east-west wooded draw. It wasn't easy. Where alders grew at all they tended to grow like giant porcupine quills a human body had a time fitting between. That was doubtless why some called such thicket's "alder hells," and back home in the wetter slopes of West-by-God-Virginia, alder hells got big enough and thick enough to trap and kill a lost stranger much the way a sundew plant could trap and kill an unwary hover fly. But out this way in dried country the springy broom-handle trees didn't slow him down that much, and he began to miss the hell out of them as soon as they petered out to leave him moving along a damned old sandy wash with his Winchester at port arms, chambered and cocked.

He hadn't gotten near enough west when even that meager cover petered out on him and he had to belly-flop and crawl up a damned old grassy rise, aiming for the half-ass cover of some rabbit bush and soap weed along the crest above him.

He took off his hat and risked a look-see between two clumps. He saw that he and McBride had been right about the source of all that smoke talk. Nobody seemed to be smoke-talking just then, but he could make out the fainter shimmer of rising smoke nobody had tossed wet grass on yet. He couldn't say whether that meant a pause in the conversation or whether the conversation was over. Before he could work out the best way to work around to the far side from where he lay, he saw someone else already had. A trim red figure on a spunky gray pony was tearing along the skyline fit to bust with a free hand upraised in the High Plains peace sign. Tupombi was too far out for him to hail. But he could hear her distant squawks as she charged the wispy column of blue smoke, and he surmised from all those *"Ka!"* sounds she was requesting somebody hold their damned fire.

Hoping to draw at least some of the fire his own way, since he knew he was way out of range, Longarm broke cover to wave his hat and yell pleas and curses at all concerned.

Tupombi spied him and be saw her wave back. But she never reined in until she'd made it to the very rise that smoke was coming from. When Longarm saw she was still alive, staring all about as she sat her reined-in pony that close to the smoke column, he muttered, "Aw, shit." and headed over to join her there.

It took a spell, crossing more than one grassy draw afoot, and then they were close enough to converse. So he called out, without breaking stride, "Thanks a heap. I was out to catch 'em, not spook 'em all the way back to the Snake River. What got into you, girl?"

She called back archly, "You, my big strong *skookumchuk*. I did not want them to kill you. That was what I was shouting just now."

He trudged on up to her, muttering, "I wish you hadn't. I was trying to sneak up on 'em."

To which she rather smugly replied, "Don't be silly. You are not a real person, as pretty as you are. My mother's people sneak up on your kind. It's not supposed to work the other way around."

He lowered the hammer of his Winchester, but swept the horizon around them with his thoughtful eyes as he muttered, "I reckon you never heard tell of Roger's Rangers, clean back in the French and Indian Wars, or Sullivan hitting those Mohawk towns like a row of dominoes on orders from General Washington. Some of our own boys talk as overconfidently about riders from back East too, forgetting where the steeplechase and thoroughbred racing was invented."

He stepped around her pony for a better view of the dying signal fire. He'd been right about them burning mostly grass with a couple of cow chips to keep it going. There was little more than a pile of smoldering gray ash now. The chalky limestone rocks laid out all across the rise were at least as interesting. Some were out of place or half hidden by weeds, but one could still make out the wheel-like pattern, about twenty yards across, as if a monstrous stone wagon had busted down up here one time.

When he asked if she knew what it meant, Tupombi shook her braided head and said, "No. I have seen *puha* like this on the other side of the Shining Mountains, but they were not made by my mother's people. So I don't know what they mean."

When he mused aloud about medicine wheels he'd seen himself, in the company of other Horse Indians who couldn't say who'd made them or why, Tupombi suggested, "You'd better get up on this horse with me. There is a smell of rain in the air and we are far from shelter over this way."

He sniffed the freshening breeze and allowed she could be right, despite the way old Tanapah still shone. Then he sniffed some more and told her, "Hold the thought. There's somebody dead around here."

Tupombi looked away, murmuring, "I was hoping you might not notice. Maybe it's just an old coyote. In any case this is a *puha* place and it's bad *puha* to bother anything that's been dead that long!"

He started walking into the breeze, searching for the source of the stink as he insisted, "I'm *paid* to pester dead folk who've died mysteriously and that's no *critter* lying dead just upwind. It only takes one war to teach one's nose the difference and . . . Yonder."

Tupombi rode no closer as Longarm stalked over to a pile of dried brush wedged against the wind between two clumps of greener soap weed. When he got there he saw someone had kicked a few bushels of dirt over the remains as well. But the dry, almost constant winds had exposed two withered feet, clad in black silk stockings, and a more horrible sight at the other end, where most of the moldering head lay exposed.

There was no way to say whether the woman had been young or old. What was left of her maggot-eaten face was just plain ugly. Her hair, a sort of mousy brown, was still pinned neatly atop her skull. A glint of gold caught his eye, even as he was trying not to puke. So he dropped to one knee beside the rotting remains to gingerly move some weed stems aside and gently finger the little heart-shaped locket the dead woman had been wearing under a summer-weight bodice of fake black silk. Real silk wouldn't have tattered so soon. Longarm got a good grip on the evidence and said, "I'm sorry, ma'am. But nobody is ever going to identify you on your looks alone, no offense, and they seem to have overlooked this personal item someone who knew you in life might recall."

He gave a good yank. The gold-washed chain of mild steel was a good deal more solid than the soggy cartilage of her spinal column. So he had to say he was sorry again when her head fell off.

He rose to his feet, letting the still-solid chain dangle as he opened the tiny heart. There were tiny tintypes inside of a silly-looking young gent and a plain young gal with her hair piled the same way. Heading back to where Tupombi still sat her pony, Longarm called out, "I think I just found one of the missing Scotch spinster gals. If you'd like to carry me back to where I left my own mount, we'll rejoin the others and see about a waterproof tarp to wrap her in."

Tupombi looked startled and asked why. He said, "Because she's dead and starting to fall apart, of course. I ain't being all that sentimental, albeit her own kith and kin would doubtless want her buried Christian rather than scattered across open range. I want some doc to look her over and see if he can figure out how she wound up so disgusting when all she came looking for was a Mormon husband."

Tupombi asked, "Does it really matter how those Shoshoni might have killed her?"

He answered, "I'm still working on who might have killed her. I doubt the ones sending smoke signals from nearby did it. I figure she's been dead close to a month. It's hard to say exactly when a body's been covered over and then exposed for unknown intervals. At any rate, them old boys you just chased away from here with all that yelling couldn't have laid out yonder medicine wheel either. So they might not have known anything about her at all."

The pretty Comanche breed smiled radiantly down at him as she said, "I see why the Utes call you Saltu Ka Saltu, Custis. I would hate to have you after me if I had done something bad. But I know you would never say bad things about me if I was innocent, whether I was Ho or Taibo."

Chapter 12

Nobody else wanted to look at the dead woman when Longarm and his grim discovery caught up with the main column an hour and change later. He'd wrapped the soggy remains in a double layer of rubberized canvas, secured with rawhide latigo, but it still managed to spook stock within a dozen yards. So he had to ride lonesome, off to one side of the trail, downwind, leading a mighty pissed-off pack brute with the dead lady aboard.

Hence he didn't hear half the mutterings that must have transpired before Tim McBride, now riding alone on point, called dinner break in a watered draw.

It was Tupombi who joined Longarm downwind of the others as he was tethering his ponies to some bare chokecherries. She'd dismounted and buried her face in his open vest before he could ask why she seemed so weepy.

She sobbed, "We're turning back. Madame Marvella was already making an awful fuss before you proved her right about dead white women around here. Shoshoni Sam said there's just time to make it back to town before dark if we leave right away. But Custis, my *Taibo skookumchuk,* I don't want to leave you, ever, ever!"

He held her gently as he softly said, "I've grown sort of used to your sweet company as well, honey. I'd be lying if I said I was pleased by the notion of you and your pals turning

141

back. But Madame Marvella has a point, and I'd be lying if I promised you anything once this mission's over. I know I ought to be whipped with snakes, but a tumbleweed job like mine just keeps me from making promises to anyone, no matter how warm I feel to 'em."

She said she understood, and asked if they couldn't part with sweeter sorrow up the draw in deeper brush. He was sorely tempted, dumb as it might have been, but then Madame Marvella yelled for Tupombi from somewhere else amid the trees. So Longarm sighed, settled for a brotherly kiss, and led the reluctant gal and her pony back to the others, saying, "I got a favor to ask of your boss, seeing he's headed back to the county seat."

Tupombi murmured back, "I don't have to do everything they say and maybe Pocatello's band would take me in, up at Fort Hall, after you don't want me anymore."

He told her not to talk silly. So she simmered down, and then it was Shoshoni Sam's turn to tell Longarm he was talking silly when, over by the cookfire, Longarm told the old showman what he wanted.

In the end, of course, the show folk headed back to the county seat, and the county coroner, with Tupombi and the dead gal, each of whom Longarm found so interesting in her own distinctive way.

Everyone else in the northbound party seemed mighty relieved. Senator Rumford said he was anxious to make up the lost time, smoke signals or not. So they pushed on harder, with riders scouting well out on all flanks as the country kept getting more open. There were double pickets the one night they had to camp out, at Longarm's suggestion, on a timbered rise, surrounded by open grassy slopes, with no fire.

Senator Rumford wanted to push on, insisting they were not that far from Fort Hall and that nobody could scout them at any distance in the dark.

Tim McBride backed him, although with some hesitation, pointing out they'd likely be smack on top of the fool

Shoshoni by daybreak and that pushing the stock that hard, through cool night air, would be safe as long as they were near the end of the drive.

But Longarm snorted and said, "I thought you said you'd spent some time in this high country, Tim. I wouldn't bet on whether we face rain, snow, or worse this side of sunrise, but that Comanche gal we left back yonder agreed with me earlier we could be in for what her kind call *waigon* weather."

He saw neither man seemed to understand and added, "*Waigon* is the Thunder Bird in Ho. Whether we ride into Fort Hall in sunshine or soaking wet, we don't *want* to surprise any Indians. The Shoshoni in particular have grim memories of white men barging in on 'em by the dawn's early light. Pocatello must be expecting us, seeing he asked for all that silver we've been packing in to him. But those smoke signals may mean other factions ain't as friendly and, like I said—"

"Don't you think Shoshoni killed that woman back near that old medicine wheel?" Tim McBride asked.

Longarm shrugged and replied, "Can't say *who* killed her before I find out. Sticking to the little we really know, we don't know shit about the reception we can expect up the trail ahead. I just said all them Indians may not agree with Pocatello about Shoshoni real estate. It can take as few at two Indians to express a dozen opinions on anything. They're not that much different from us, and after that, we still don't know those smoke signals were meant to be all that sinister. I know they puffed at us, and others before us. Meanwhile, there's no proof any Indian is on the warpath, and we could all be spooking at neighborhood gossip."

Senator Rumford grumbled, "I wish you'd make up your mind. First you say we'd best move in cautiously, and then you point out there may be no trouble at all!"

Longarm nodded soberly and said, "It's best to keep both options open in Indian country, Senator. I could tell you tales of overconfident gents waking up dead and bald whilst, at the same time, grim things have happened to Indians who

143

didn't know they were on the warpath till they heard bugles blowing and field guns blasting. So unless you'd like to claim that Indian land the old-fashioned way, from dead Indians, it might be best to ride in sedately, well after sunrise, after Pocatello's scouts have had time to announce our visit."

Senator Rumford grumped off in the darkness to fuss at someone else while Longarm, McBride, and other natural leaders drifting in worked out the best way to get them all through the night.

Since they'd already agreed on the site and cold suppers, there was little more than the details left to work out. Longarm didn't like to sound bossy, as long as he was getting his own way on important matters. So he just leaned against a tree and smoked as the others decided who'd pull guard, with whom, and where. Longarm had already noticed the fair-sized outfit had sort of split into three more or less friendly factions, based on natural feelings. Aside from the quartet of older gents from the congressional delegation, the eight or ten Western riders split without obvious rancor into those who'd worked with McBride and Pearson before and those who'd worked at other Indian agencies or other outfits. So nobody fussed, and Longarm just went on smoking, when McBride and young Jeffries, off the Rosebud Reserve, decided it worked best if the congressmen, led by Longarm, took first watch, Jeffries and his bunch took second, and McBride and the others off the White River Agency worried about the wee small hours.

Having agreed on that, they secured all the stock downwind, with the packs, including all that silver specie, smack in the center of camp so everyone would bed down all about it. By the time they'd all eaten uncooked canned goods it was dark enough to make them wonder where the damned moon might be. Longarm wasn't the only one to notice there were no stars out either, and surmise a mess of clouds up yonder.

Pulling first watch, glad as hell he was wearing a frock coat and vest as he drifted through the trees with his Winchester, dying for a smoke he dared not light, Longarm found his inner thoughts more interesting than the almost pitch blackness all about him.

He'd elected to circle farther out, suspecting the others on this watch, being the greener apples in this barrel, would stick closer to their bedrolls than they ought to. So he had mostly open slopes to his left, the way his cradled Winchester pointed, as he circled clockwise along the ragged tree line. He couldn't see shit on such an overcast night, of course. But he felt safer when it began to snow. He knew no Indian night crawler with any brains would crawl far enough to matter in even a light snowfall. The idea of night crawling was to hit and run, not leave a trail even a schoolmarm could follow come daybreak.

Halfway through his watch he went back to his own bedroll to break out his oilcloth slicker. The damned snowfall was warm enough to melt into tweed instead of brushing off. He caught Congressman Granger fucking off in another bedroll, but didn't fuss when the older asshole said something dumb about having a lung condition. Granger wouldn't have been any more use out on picket, and at least he lay there in the way of anyone coming after the piled packs in the middle of camp. The others were naturally bedded down on the other sides. Some of them were already snoring. It was commencing to snow harder by the time Longarm was back along the tree line wrapped up in his crunchy poplin and linseed oil slicker. He was tempted to smoke, knowing nobody could see any better amid the swirls of invisible snow. But he didn't. He'd learned as a soldier in his teens that night picket was either tedious as hell or more exciting than you'd really planned on, and it had always been the pickets who'd been certain it was safe to fuck off who'd been nailed in the dark when it hadn't been.

So he kept doing it right, dull as it felt, with the snow now deep enough to crunch under his boots, inspiring him to circle a mite slower, his bored brain racing in circles as it considered all his recent adventures and tried to make some sensible pattern out of them.

Nothing sensible seemed to work. Plodding on, trying not to think about some other recent adventures lest he have to plod on through wind and snow with a full erection, Longarm managed to come up with a few really wild patterns. He knew the head docs had a name for a poor soul who took every possible plot against him as probable. So he decided that while it was *possible* some kith or kin of that rich pain in the ass he'd shot back in Denver had it in for him, there was simply no way in hell old W. R. Callisher's friends or relations could have killed that lady of the little locket—long before he'd shot Callisher, from the smell of her.

The same reasoning let everyone connected with this expedition off the same hook, even Pearly, The Kid, and their mysterious Pappy, as soon as one considered how long Scotch spinster gals had been vanishing in these parts.

"Back up," he warned himself aloud. "You don't know that poor lady of the locket was one of them vanished Scotch spinsters till you show her locket to someone who can say for certain. For all you really know she was a happily married Bulgarian, or far more likely a Mormon homestead gal killed, or mayhaps just left out there, by . . . Aw, shit, this ain't getting us nowhere and we need more damned *facts*!"

The wet swirling winds didn't offer any. They just kept getting wetter. The damned snow was starting to mix with rain by the time Longarm decided it was time to wake young Jeffries and his watch.

When he got back to the snow-covered pile-up on the crest of the rise, he found all the damned dudes had beaten him under the covers. He was more disgusted than annoyed when Senator Rumford told him Jeffries and his own bunch had already gotten up and moved out through the trees.

Longarm peeled out of his slicker and slipped into his own roll before he could get wet, taking off the bumpier stuff as he lay under the waterproof top tarp. It wasn't easy to get comfortable. But it had been a long day, not even counting the earlier screwing, so the next thing he knew he was screwing a Scotch spinster on a big plaid-covered bedstead by broad day while Dame Flora and her maidservant made snide comments and old Angus played on a bagpipe.

Then, before he could come, he was wide awake—that always seemed to happen, dammit—and he saw it was bright moonlight, not broad daylight, he'd been screwing in buck naked. So now he was back in his rumpled shirt and pants, needing to piss, and what time was it?

He propped himself up on one elbow, wiping the sleep gum from his eyes with his free hand before he groped for his watch in the duds he'd been using as a pillow. It was four in the morning. He'd have likely made it till morning, he felt sure, had not that break in the storm conspired with his kidneys to wake him so early, and if he could just fall back to sleep quickly, he might not have to crawl out of this nice warm roll just yet and . . .

"Aw, shit, let's get it over with," he decided, tossing a flap of tarp aside to haul himself on out. He saw everyone around lay dead to the world in the moonlight as he hauled his boots on over his socks. He figured right McBride and Pearson would be on watch with their bunch at this hour. He didn't call out to them lest he disturb the others closer. He reached for his Winchester, without having to think about it, and rose to find a politer place to piss.

That was easy enough to decide on, since he already knew where the stock was tethered, downwind. He naturally wanted to piss on the far side of the stock. He might have spooked them passing too close in tricky light. So he circled wide, on rain-soaked pine duff one could have crossed silently in Dutch clogs, and nobody knew he was there as he heard Pearson insisting, "I say now's the time. It'll soon be light again, and you know that son of a bitch can get those son-of-a-bitching Shoshoni to track us if he asks 'em to!"

Longarm forgot about pissing as he flattened his shadowy shape against a pine just as the voice of McBride replied, "I know what the Indians will do for a Saltu they trust. That's why I say we've got to do him before we light out. None of the others can do shit once we're over a rise or more, but that savvy bastard's got to die here and now!"

Longarm was pretty certain he knew who they were talking about before he heard Pearson protest, "It's too big a boo, Pappy. You can't gun a man in the middle of a camp, in tricky light, without risking all sorts of return fire!"

McBride said, "Bullshit. The sky's cleared entire and that moon is shining almost bright as an overcast day. I can see all of you plain as hell now,"

Longarm broke cover to throw down on the four of them from the hip, levering a round into the chamber to let them know he was a force to be reckoned with as he said conversationally, "Pappy is right, gents. I can almost see the whites of your fucking eyes. So raise them fucking hands and raise 'em *now*!"

Two Agency teamsters did. McBride tried to swing the muzzle of his own saddle gun in line while Duke Pearson simply bolted, bleating like a sheep, so Longarm blew McBride off his feet before he swung the smoking muzzle of his Winchester the other way to nail the bolting breed in the small of his back. You could tell it was a shithouse-lucky spine-shot by the way his hat soared skyward while he landed on his face in an oddly graceful swan dive.

Longarm swung his muzzle back to cover the remaining members of the plot. He saw he'd done right and fired again, folding the one who'd dropped his hands, his six-gun still holstered as his numbed right hand let go of the grips. As he finished falling to the soggy duff, the only one still on his feet clawed wildly at the moon above them, sobbing, "Please don't do me, Longarm! I was only working for 'em. I swear I never done nothing really bad to nobody!"

Longarm told him to unbuckle his gun rig and step clear of the results as he moved in on the fallen McBride, Winchester trained. McBride was sort of writhing about, like an earthworm caught by a sunrise on a brick walk. So Longarm asked not unkindly, "How are you feeling, Pappy?"

The treacherous Indian agent groaned, "Awful. Who told on us, you sly rascal? I knew from the beginning you were good, but this seems plain ridiculous!"

Longarm heard other voices calling out in the dark and yelled back, "Over this way, gents. Watch out you don't spook any pack mules you may stumble over. I just caught me some silver thieves and a heap of answers here!"

McBride croaked, "No shit, I need a doc. I fear you've killed me, you fucker!"

To which Longarm replied in an amiable tone, "I was aiming to kill you when I shot you. It seemed only fair, considering."

Then he turned to the one unscathed survivor, adding, "I reckon you'll be able to tie up all the loose ends for us. Westmore, ain't it?"

"Don't tell him shit!" McBride croaked from the ground as they were joined by old Rumford, young Jeffries, and the others. So Longarm said, "I wish you'd just shut up and die, Pappy. Westmore here has to tell us everything he knows because he doesn't want to hang. Ain't that right, Westmore?"

The younger teamster stammered, "Hang? For what? Every time we tried to kill you one of *us* wound up dead, but all right, I may as well tell you all I know, you murderous cuss!"

Chapter 13

Westmore did, more than once, with two congressmen and a mess of more honest riders to bear witness. But as was so often the case, the simple enough plot of a corrupt Indian agent and his not-too-bright recruits only formed one gear wheel of what seemed more like a cuckoo clock when you really studied on it.

Westmore confessed, after all his pals had finished dying, that he'd been part of a vicious but uncomplicated plan to make off with all those untraceable silver dollars. Westmore said the brains of the gang, if one wanted to call him that, had been Tim McBride, known as Pappy to his junior crooks. Making off with the Shoshoni silver had occurred to McBride as soon as he'd been asked by the B.I.A. to escort the congressmen and act as their translator. McBride, in turn, had recruited Duke Pearson, who could actually speak Ho. The B.I.A. was always taking some flea-brain's word that he was a real expert with Indians, Longarm thought.

The lesser thugs, recruited as easily in turn, had included boys lying in wait for Longarm as well as those fake scouts who'd been out to make sure he never joined up with the expedition.

When Senator Rumford wanted to know why, Westmore stared sadly at Longarm to reply, "Jesus H. Christ, what a dumb question! Pappy knew Longarm here would be harder to outfox than all the rest of you put together. Didn't he just prove that? Don't the Utes call him by pet names because he busted up an Indian Ring that had half the Indians and all of the whites fooled? Pappy had worked under gents of the Grant Administration Longarm and others like him had put in jail. When he heard the B.I.A. had fucked him up by asking for a man the Indians trusted even more, he knew he had to get rid of Longarm or let the damned Shoshoni have their damned silver!"

Longarm warned, "You're talking in circles. I know how Pearson scared off those other Ho-speaking scouts, talking Ho to 'em behind some backs. Get to those smoke signals and the dead woman I found so close to that medicine wheel."

Westmore seemed sincerely confused as he insisted, "Not a one of us knew shit about any of that stuff. I swear none of us killed any old white gal. I was riding next to Duke when he first spied them smoke signals. He was surprised as the rest of us. I don't think Pappy knew anything about 'em neither!"

Longarm nodded soberly and decided, "If he did, he was sure a born actor. I think he went along with me on that stuff because he accepted it at face value, same as the rest of us. He was looking for no more than a crack at grabbing all that silver and running for it, through the mountains to the east he likely knew better than the rest of you gents, no offense. So we keep on getting back to other plotters, red, white, or both."

Young Jeffries opined it seemed obvious Indians had killed that Scotch spinster over by the Indian medicine wheel. So Longarm had to ask if anyone there had ever heard of a Quill Indian placing proposals of marriage in your average Scotch newspaper.

They all agreed it was a poser. Then, since by then they were all wide awake and the sky to the east was pearling gray, they ate, broke camp, and were on their way, with the tarp-wrapped corpses lashed across their own saddles and Westmore being led aboard his pony with both hands cuffed behind his back.

When he protested he'd surely fall off and bust his neck if his pony burst into full gallop, Longarm suggested dryly he try not to gallop off anywhere.

Having left Zion so late the day before, they'd had to camp less than halfway to Fort Hall. So they had a full day's ride ahead of them. But the weather held just right for rapid progress as the country around kept getting safer-looking.

The stock moved frisky because the overnight storm had left a cool tang in the air and drinking water at most every trail break. The same gray skies that kept the sun from warming them up too much were an inspiration to take short breaks and push on, lest another early snow catch them out in the middle of nowhere.

As for the country, the swells all about got flatter and further apart as they rode ever closer to the Snake River Plains up ahead. Some rises overlooking the trail sprouted more evergreen timber than Longarm really cottoned to, so those had to be scouted before the mules packing so much temptation passed within rifle range. But at least they saw no more smoke signals, which was tougher for the surviving crook to explain, and led some others to mutter mean things about his veracity.

But they were too busy to question him enough to matter. Thanks to the shoot-out having left them short-handed, even the politicians from back East had to pitch in and help with the pack mules and saddle swapping chores. But Longarm was glad to see they were good sports about it, and some of his more Western companions might have learned something as well. Older gents who'd gone into politics had all been younger gents doing something else in their time, and folks east and west had to know something about horses in a horse-drawn age. The sort of soft and sissy-looking Congressman Granger turned out to be a born mule skinner, or at any rate a man who'd plowed a fair farrow behind his own daddy's mules as a boy.

Hence the long day on the trail passed without any noteworthy problems, and along about five, when they finally did see Indians on a rise ahead, Longarm told his companions those hand-me-down army blues most of them had on meant they were Indian Police off some nearby agency. When Senator Rumford observed the only agency in those parts was the one at Fort Hall, Longarm said that was what he meant.

As the Shoshoni met them on the rise, an English-speaking Corporal Shoogan in command of the eight in uniform, the other dozen being free thinkers who'd just tagged along, told them they were a mite overdue as well as welcome. When Senator Rumford demanded to know how far they were from the Fort Hall Shoshoni-Bannock Reservation, the moon-faced Shoogan told him, "You've been on it for some time. We are still a great nation and all the hunting grounds you see around you, all, are still our hunting grounds. Even Little Big Eyes in Washington will tell you this is so."

Longarm explained the senator had meant the agency itself. So Shoogan pointed north and said. "This side of sundown, if you Taibo would like to cut this bullshit and ride."

They rode. The modern agency built more or less on the site of the original fortified trading post lay well their side of sundown, surrounding a tall sun-bleached flagstaff with the well-weathered Stars and Stripes still flapping in the last light of the day.

By this time Longarm had brought Corporal Shoogan up to date on his own problems. Shoogan told him they'd be proud to hold Westmore as long as need be in their swell jail and that, yes, they had a talking wire running east along the old wagon route, if Longarm could get one of the Taibo at the agency to work such a strange *ahotey* for him.

When Senator Rumford asked whether they'd find Chief Pocatello in one of the low-slung log or sun-silvered frame structures they could see ahead now, Shoogan snorted, "Of course not. Pocatello is our Powamu Puhahow! What would he be doing in our jail, dispensary, or working for the Taibo with other household help? Hear me, Pocatello has his own cabin, a big one, on a bend of our big river where the fishing is always good!"

154

Rumford asked how, in that case, he was supposed to meet with Pocatello and his sub-chiefs to talk about real estate. Shoogan shook his head and said, "Tomorrow, maybe, after you and all your friends have had time to bathe and change your clothes as guests of the agency. Hear me, you will want to get some sleep, a lot of sleep, before you meet with our tribal council in the morning, if it doesn't rain. Every *powamu* there will want to make a speech, a long speech, and you will be expected to listen respectfully to every word, even though most of them don't speak a word of Taibo."

For some reason, that didn't seem to cheer up the gents from back East worth mentioning. Longarm kept his own council amid all the confusing jabber until they'd all reined in out front of the main agency building, where the Shoshoni-Bannock agent and other whites were lined up along the veranda to greet them. More than one face in the crowd looked familiar, and Longarm was glad. But he waited till he and the Indian Police were leading Westmore over to the nearby lockup before he asked Shoogan when Dame Flora and her two servants had made it in.

The Shoshoni said, "Yesterday, on lathered ponies. They said they had seen smoke talk and felt afraid. The flame-haired woman who has such a high opinion of herself told us they were looking for Taibo women who came far, far, to marry Mormons. This was a stupid place to look for such stupid women, if you ask me. We told her we didn't know anything about it. She said everyone she talks to keeps telling her that. I am glad I don't have such a woman. I would have to beat her all the time if I ever wanted to eat. All she does is talk, talk, talk about other stupid women nobody knows."

Westmore wanted to talk some more as Longarm handed him a couple of smokes, warned him he'd best make them last, and said he'd let him know, later, where the powers that be might want him delivered to stand trial and for what. When Westmore intimated he might be able to suggest some angles on that dead lady Longarm had found near the medicine ring,

Longarm told him it was a mite late and that he meant to ask some Indians.

He wasn't surprised when, stepping back outside with Shoogan, he learned the Agaiduka Shoshoni didn't know much more than he did about those mysterious stone circles. Shoogan said he'd heard a mysterious people called the Tukaduka had laid out medicine wheels for mysterious reasons, back before Spider Woman had led the first Ho into this world from somewhere more mysterious.

As he started to untether his hired paint from the hitching rail out front, Longarm paused thoughtfully and said, "One of those crooks you said you'd store in that springhouse for us answered to Duke and spoke Ho fluently. So run that Tukaduka by me again, pard."

Shoogan shrugged and said, "Tukaduka just means sheep-eaters. I don't know why our old ones called the ones who were here before us sheep-eaters, but they did."

Longarm decided, "Somebody must have noticed 'em eating sheep, likely wild bighorn sheep if we're talking about way back when. And ancient folks who nailed enough mountain sheep to matter with no more than bows and arrows would rate *my* admiration as well. So might *tuka* or *duka* mean what?"

Shoogan said, "*Tuka* means sheep. *Duka* means those who eat. What are we talking about?"

Longarm shrugged and replied, "Likely nothing. Old Duke did eat lots of grub. But even if that was how he got his nickname, I can't connect him up with any Tukaduka medicine wheel, and I doubt lost tribes were sending smoke signals down that way in any case."

He mounted up, resisting the impulse to ask a Shoshoni whether the ancient Tukaduka might have practiced human sacrifice, the way the Pawnee had before they'd given it up without being asked. A lawman who asked questions for a living learned not to ask them of folk who couldn't know the answers.

156

He rode the short distance back to the main agency building, and dismounted near the roan he'd left there with other tethered ponies. He switched saddles out there in the gathering darkness in case he wanted to head out soon aboard a fresher mount. Then he mounted the plank steps and strode on into the good-sized main hall, where he found his own dudes flustering around Dame Flora MacSorley by the baronial stone fireplace where a pitch-pine fire was acting sort of frisky this evening as well.

Senator Rumford called him over and introduced him to both the Scotch lady he already knew and a far homelier middle-aged Indian agent of the male persuasion. When Longarm explained where he'd just been, the agent suggested he head on back to the dining room and tell the squaws to rustle him a late snack, explaining, "You just missed a simple but hearty serving of planked salmon and home fries with serviceberry pie."

Longarm said he'd do that. He didn't feel up to explaining why he'd had to finish his chores first to an asshole who called his own Shoshoni women squaws, as if they'd been Arapaho. Dudes such as Dame Flora and the senator had excuses for not bothering with any Indian lingo. But you'd think a cuss getting paid to look after Shoshoni would learn at least a few simple words.

As Longarm strode off, the senator called something about a big powwow with Pocatello in the morning. Longarm didn't care. He was more surprised, and not too happy about it, when the auburn-haired Dame Flora chased him clean out of the room, saying, "Wait for me. They just told me you found the remains of a white woman."

He said, "Sent her in to the county seat for the coroner to do something with her. I was fixing to mention her to you later, on a less uncertain stomach. Whether she was one of your missing gals or not, she wasn't a topic I'd want to take up over a meal."

But Dame Flora had already eaten, or maybe had had time to get more interested in the topic. So she tagged right along, insisting they'd told her about that infernal locket. So as they entered the smaller dining room, where a couple of Shoshoni *pias* were clearing the long table by lamplight, Longarm got out the small gold-washed locket to hand over to the pretty but sort of pesky Dame Flora.

One of the Indian gals came over, hesitantly, as if to see what they wanted. Longarm tried to tell her in English, and when that didn't work he patted his belly and tried, "*Duka.* Me *ka duka* this evening, ma'am."

It worked. She brightened, blew Shoshoni bubbles at him, and commenced to lead him off with her as Dame Flora suddenly sobbed, "*Och, cha 'n'eil!* But it is! It was poor little Una Munro you found murdered and scalped by Indians down the trail, and we three must have ridden right past her remains!"

He tagged after the Shoshoni gal, with the Scotch gal after him, as he explained, "She hadn't been scalped, or even stripped now that you mention it, and we found her half buried a good ways off the trail, ma'am. Never would have found her at all had not I been scouting others who might or might not have been the ones who put her there."

By then they were back in the darker, steamier kitchen, where the waitress gal was sort of chanting in Ho at an older and far fatter gal who shot Longarm a dirty look and finally managed to convey, in words he couldn't quite follow and hand signs he knew better, that she was willing to rustle him up some grub if he didn't expect cheese with his pie, Taiowa damn it.

He signed back that coffee and sandwiches would be fine with him as Dame Flora kept pestering him about rotting corpses. He led her over to a corner where they'd be out of the way as he told her "I don't *know* why any Indians would murder an unarmed immigrant gal and not even take her pretty locket. She could have lost her shoes most anywhere. I don't see how Shoshoni sending smoke signals that close to where she lay could have known she was there. I might not have, had the wind been blowing another way. Most folks

158

who've hidden a body a good ways off on open range try not to attract attention to it. Soon as I wrap myself around some coffee and grub I mean to go ask some Shoshoni about those Shoshoni smoke signals."

She asked what made him so certain they'd been Shoshoni. The fat old gal was coming their way with a mug of coffee and a plate piled high with corn *piki* and salmon sandwiches. So Longarm told the Scotch gal, "Because Bannock don't ride that far south and Paiute are afraid to come that far north. Now hush and let me talk to this Shoshoni lady."

They both seemed mildly surprised when Longarm thanked the fat gal by extending both hands, palms down, and sweeping them low like some fool pagan praying to some idol. Then he set the mug and sandwiches aside on a corner of her cast-iron range, to leave both hands free as he tried to ask directions to the lodge of her Chief Pocatello. It wasn't easy, and he had a time following her directions once she seemed to follow his drift.

It helped him as well as Dame Flora if he repeated the meanings of each sign in English. So when the fat gal raised her pudgy hand, fingers spread, and pivoted it on her wrist he muttered, "Wants to ask a question." He told her to go ahead and ask, with his own fist near his mouth, fingers opening and closing.

She pointed at him, drew her palm across her own brow, made it snake-slither, then put her fist to her heart before she put the back of it to her lips with the index finger pointed at him. So he said, "I think she's asking if I might be the white man they call the one with a Shoshoni heart."

Then he modestly said, *"Ayee,"* knowing that meant yes in Ho, and so she grabbed him in a happy bear hug and began to yell fit to bust until a Shoshoni boy came in from out back with a broom and a puzzled expression. He spoke English. So it was easier for him to say, "Aunt Tahcutiney wants me to lead you over to our big chief's cabin, Taibo with Our Kind of Heart."

Longarm said that sounded swell, gulped some coffee, and

159

grabbed the sandwich off the plate to eat on the fly as he followed the boy out the back door with Dame Flora still following *him*. It was dark as an overcast night figured to get outside by this time. When he asked the Shoshoni boy whether they'd be walking or riding, the boy said he was walking and that it wasn't too far for a real man. So Longarm said to just lead on, but warned the Scotch gal in high-buttons she'd likely be more comfortable just waiting inside till he returned.

She said she wasn't about to sit and fidget now that they were so close, at last, to some answers about those missing spinsters.

He told her, "Ain't sure how close we might be to anything right now. Not even where we might be heading. So don't say I never warned you and don't expect us to carry you if you can't keep up."

She said she wouldn't. As they crunched along over uncertain footing after the barely visible outline of the young Shoshoni, she asked him why he didn't like her.

When he said he liked her as much as anyone else he knew around Fort Hall, she said she wasn't used to being spoken to so curtly by her social inferiors.

To which he could only reply with a wry chuckle, "I'd already got that feeling about you, ma'am. Mayhaps that's what inspired me to keep things plain and simple. If it's any comfort to you, I ain't your social inferior. I'm a born and bred American from West-by-God-Virginia, and my ancestors whupped your ancestors twice."

She hissed like a stomped sidewinder, muttered something awful in Gaelic, then laughed despite herself and said, "I'll have you know it was the Sasunnach, I mean the English, you colonists had so much fun with. But your point's well taken, so lead on, Mo MacNial na Barra."

Longarm answered, simply, "Can't. If this kid ain't leading us the right way we're lost, and who's that other cuss you seem to have me mixed up with, ma'am?"

She laughed again and said, "Mixed up indeed. The

160

MacNial, the high chief of a small but proud island clan, was invited to court by one of our German Georges, but since he'd arrived in the rain with his tartan plaid wrapped around him and the eagle feathers drooping on his wet blue bonnet, he was lucky to get any place at the king's table at all. You know, of course, that guests are seated beginning at the head of the table in order of rank?"

He said he'd heard as much, complicated as it sounded. So she explained, "The MacNial was seated below the salt, or near the unfashionable end of the table, among mere Sirs and even Right Honorables. Being a true Highland gentleman he said nothing but simply started eating, with his hat still on, in the Highland fashion."

Longarm said, "Hebrews and cowhands too. Saves having to fuss with your fool hat before or after. Is that why I remind you of this cuss, because I've been chawing on this sandwich with my hat on all this time?"

She said, "No. You see, after a time the king, at the head of his table, noticed the chief's four feathers, sensed they might mean something, and had one of his servants make some discreet inquires. One can imagine His Majesty's chagrin when it developed they'd seated a ruler in his own right below the salt. At any rate an equerry in a white wig was sent down to The MacNial to offer a full apology and move such a distinguished guest up by the head of the table. But by then the chief had started eating and so all he did was glance up to shout, the length of the table, 'Och, dinna' frush yersel', Gordie. Wherever The MacNial may be seated already *is* the head of the table!' "

Longarm didn't laugh. He swallowed the last of his slim supper and said, "Makes sense to me. I don't see what all the frush was about neither."

She replied, in a softer tone, "That's what I meant. I think I see why the Indians call you a white man with an Indian heart. They seem to see things less, well, frushy than the rest of us."

He sighed and said, "Don't bank on that, ma'am. They mean I try to understand them, not that they can't act just as complicated, as you'll see once we meet up with some of 'em, if ever we meet up with *any* of 'em."

He managed not to pester their silent and almost invisible Indian guide until, somewhere in the night, they heard someone singing in a high-pitched but sleepy-sounding way. Then they saw faint lights ahead and their young guide called out. The singing stopped. Then a male voice called back in Ho, and the kid told Longarm and Dame Flora, "Pocatello makes you welcome if you come with good hearts and don't want to sell him anything."

Longarm said that sounded fair. So the kid yelled some more and then they headed on in. When she saw about a dozen blanket-wrapped forms seated cross-legged on the front porch of a log cabin, back-lit by an oil lamp on one windowsill, Dame Flora marveled, "Why, they seem to living in a real house, as if they were white people."

He said, "Yes, ma'am. It gets cold as a banker's heart up this way come January, so would *you* squat in a tipi you had to put up yourself when the government was willing to build you a fine cabin?"

She dimpled and said she understood. He told her to keep future comments to herself, lest folks feel she felt too good for them. He was pleased when she said she'd let him do all the talking.

But now they were close enough for the Indians on the porch to make them out as well. A bearlike figure wrapped in a cream and black-striped Hudson Bay blanket rose to a tad above average for a Ho, all Ho being shorter than your average lanky Lakota, and began a speech in a curious mishmash of English, Chinook, and Ho. Longarm gravely replied he'd been on fair terms with the late "Big Um" too, hoping they were talking about Brigham Young. Trying to introduce Dame Flora, even with sign thrown in, was a real bitch. Then a sort of sweet old female voice cut in to hush the chief and offer

162

to translate, in better English than Longarm was used to speaking.

Moving in closer, they saw she seemed to be someone's mummy, the Egyptian kind, wrapped in a real old-timey blanket made by wrapping thin strips of rabbit fur around *weepah* cords and weaving them into a sort of thick fuzzy burlap. The old woman's long hair was whiter than Pocatello's blanket. She said she was called Wadzewipa, and when the young boy from the agency said she was a *porivo,* the old gal sighed and said, "I am no such thing. I am only a guest who came over the mountains from Fort Washakie to speak for my young nephew, Pocatello, and make sure the Taibo didn't cheat him."

Longarm braced a booted foot on the porch steps and chose his words carefully before he said, "Hear me, Wadzewipa, and tell your nephew I ride with the Taibo who want to buy that land, but not as one of those who will try to set the price."

The old woman softly replied, "We know who you are. The Ute were right to name you Saltu Ka Saltu. What is it you really want from Pocatello?"

Longarm glanced at Dame Flora, sighed, and told her, "If I say I'm doing this partly for you, can you sort of forget the details of this conversation, ma'am?"

She said her kind didn't hold with idle gossip. So he turned back to the Indians and said, "I know better than to try and trade with you like a Chinook with stolen ponies. Tell Pocatello I offer this freely, as a good enemy in war and a brother in peace. Tell him my people want that land he is willing to sell them more than they may have told him. Tell him he could get at least twice as much silver if he can hold out until the crops are sprouting after the last snows."

Wadzewipa stared silently for a time before she sighed and said, "I think you know what you are talking about, my *tua.* Everyone knows how much Pocatello can buy for his people, with cold and hungry moons coming, for sixty thousand dollars."

163

"Four hundred thousand acres are worth more," Longarm told her.

She raised a frail hand to hush him, saying, "Pocatello is not going to sell them that much land. A good seventy-five thousand are *important* acres. The Taibo can have the rest. Do you think he could really get a hundred and twenty thousand dollars for, say, three hundred and twenty-five thousand acres?"

Longarm nodded and said, "Easy. They want that land more than Pocatello does, and twice what they've offered is still cheaper by far than even a modest war. All Pocatello has to remember is that they will be counting on the coming winter to weaken his resolve. The B.I.A. has to get you all through the winter alive, albeit without fancy trimmings. That's the law of the land. Come springtime, with him holding out for a halfway fair price . . ."

"*Hai-hai-yee!* Be quiet and let me tell them!" she cried with a delighted cackle. As she did so in their own lingo Dame Flora calmly asked Longarm, "What was the name of that Yankee chap who sided with the Indians against his own kind that time, Simon Girty?"

He smiled thinly and said, "You'd know better than me, since he was a British agent, ma'am. I ain't out to scalp or even slicker my side unfairly. Less than a million dollars for half that much well-watered land is a steal and you know it."

She smiled demurely and replied, "I'm beginning to think you must have some Scottish blood in you, and canny Lowlander at that. But I still don't see why you've been so free with your business advice, Custis."

He told her to just wait. So she did, and after a lot of good-natured chatter old Wadzewipa smiled up at them to announce, "We think your words are wise and that your heart is as good as our Ute cousins and favorite enemies say. My nephew wants to know if there is anything *we* can do for *you*."

There was, but they couldn't. The old woman's fifty- or sixty-year-old nephew seemed to care as she translated. But neither he nor any of the other important Shoshoni could shed light on that fool smoke talk to the south, let alone missing spinster gals. Old Wadzewipa looked mighty weepy as she sadly told them, "They know nothing, nothing, of any missing girls, and all our young men, all, are on the reservation. We told them not to do anything silly with people coming to give us so much silver. We did not know we could get even more if we held out a little longer. Pocatello says you have his word there will be no raiding, not even for chickens, until after he gets all that silver for his people!"

Longarm asked more questions anyway. While the old woman was translating, Dame Flora asked how much of the money anyone but old Pocatello was ever likely to see.

He said, "All of it. Indian politics ain't like our own. When an Indian leader robs his own people they never speak to him again, if he's awfully lucky. I don't think it would occur to a traditional, like Pocatello, to spend one dime on his personal comforts. You get to be a big chief by *acting* big."

She nodded soberly and decided, "Like the old Viking or Highland chiefs. I agree with you on bankers' hearts. It was the Sasunnach who introduced such customs to Caledonia the Wild."

Old Wadzewipa turned back to sort of sob, "They know nothing about those medicine wheels either. The Tukaduka who fashioned them are gone, all gone. I am ashamed to say it, but they know nothing about a dead woman either."

Longarm nodded grimly and told her, "I never thought Indians sending smoke signals near a dead lady they knew about made sense to begin with. You mind if I ask you a more personal question, Miss Wadzewipa?"

She told him to go on. So he said, "Some others I met down by Zion were jawing about the famous Sacajawea of the Lewis and Clark expedition. They'd been told she might still be alive, living somewhere among her own people."

Wadzewipa sighed and said, "Sacajawea means nothing, nothing, in Ho."

Longarm nodded soberly and said, "Yes, ma'am. Bird Woman is what they called her in their reports to President Jefferson. They said she was a swell translator who spoke French and Indian tolerably, and Shoshoni, of course, more fluently."

Wadzewipa sighed and said, "I know the story of Bird Woman. Some say she died a long time ago, before all her children and others she loved."

He tried gently, "They say her real name was Boinaiv, and that she never died, Umbeah."

The old woman choked back a gasp of anguish and finally croaked, "I know what is in your heart, but please don't address me as your mother. I am nobody's mother, nobody's. My *skookumchuka* have all become ghosts and it is not good to mention the names of ghosts. This grass girl of whom you speak no longer walks the earth."

He persisted gently, "We wouldn't be talking about her at all if we knew for certain she was dead, ma'am. Might you know whatever became of her in later years?"

It was Dame Flora's turn to choke back gasps as the older woman murmured, in a matter-of-fact way, "She was passed around by men, as such women are, while they are young and pretty. After a time men left her alone and maybe she was of more use at councils, having known many men of many nations, and speaking many tongues. What did these people who were asking about the grass girl of so long ago want with her, if ever they found her?"

Longarm said, "They wanted her to go into a Wild West show with them, ma'am. They thought a heap of my kind would pay lots of money to see the bird woman who led Lewis and Clark clean across the continent in the Shining Times."

The old woman didn't answer. Beside him, Dame Flora murmured, "Custis, you don't really think . . ."

But he said, "I don't know what to think. What do you think, Miss Wadzewipa? Have you ever hankered to join a Wild West show, in case I meet up with those show folk again?"

The old woman laughed incredulously and said, "*Ka!* That must be the one thing that's never happened to me, in a lifetime that has seen many happenings! Can't you just tell them Bird Woman is no more . . . my *tua*?"

He nodded and said, "Sure I can, Umbeah. Everyone with a lick of sense knows Bird Woman lies buried over at Fort Union. So it's been nice talking with you all, but now this other lady and me better get on back to the agency before they come looking for us."

Reservation Indians didn't need to have such things explained to them. So the young kitchen helper simply said he'd show Longarm and Dame Flora how to get back. As they followed him Dame Flora explained she and her servants had already been assigned to guest rooms in an out-building near the headquarters building. So Longarm figured the agency would have worked such matters out with his own party by now, and added that he hoped they didn't expect him to double up with anyone who snored.

She rather archly observed that that fat cook might not snore and certainly liked him. He'd already considered that and put it out of his mind without much strain. So he called ahead to their Ho-speaking guide, asking the kid just what the name Wadzewipa might mean.

The boy said, "Hard to say in English. Try someone who is lost, hopelessly lost, with no place to go back to."

Longarm thanked him and muttered he'd suspected it might mean something like that.

Dame Flora moved closer to murmur, "It has to be her, don't you think so, Custis?"

Longarm shrugged and replied, "Ain't paid to think about ladies who ain't done nothing wrong and just want to be left alone. They pay me to worry about ladies who've done something bad or had something bad done to them, like that lady of the locket."

"Una Munro," sighed Dame Flora, adding, "It's nice to meet such a gentleman of discretion. It's been over a year since I have, and there are times I wish I didn't have to be so discreet myself."

He asked what she had to be so discreet about, aside from her nosing high and low for those missing Scotch spinsters. But she just shot a thoughtful look at the dark outline of their Shoshoni guide and suggested they discuss it in private later.

But of course they never had to. Longarm was a man who could take a hint as well as he could keep a secret. So he hardly needed to be slapped across the face with female underdrawers when Dame Flora hung around, staring at pictures on the walls, all the time an agency clerk was telling Longarm how to find the quarters they'd assigned him in a lean-to at one end of the stables.

They'd both been around enough to know it was far more discreet for a lady to slip into a gent's private quarters late at night than vice versa. So he was expecting her before she came discreetly tapping, and had her in the bunk bed with her skirts up and drawers down before she could finish all that high-toned sophistry about a grown woman's need to keep her plumbing in working order.

She said she was glad after he'd plumbed her good. She asked him why he thought she couldn't stop talking, even after he'd made her come, hotter than she'd expected to, and proceeded to strip her down to do things right now that he, at least, felt less awkward.

He told her she was talking too much lest he ask her things she might not want him to.

She started to deny that, laughed, and decided, "You're right, and I really do find it tiresome to make up a life story no blackmailer could ever use every time I wind up in this ridiculous position. And speaking of positions, just what do you think you're trying to do with that amazing erection now, darling?"

He got a better grip on her shapely but firm horsewoman's hips as he sort of let his old organ-grinder find its own way while he told her, "We call this dog-style. Once we get you up on your hands and knees all the way, I mean."

168

She laughed and said, "You lovable lout, you can't get it in me that way unless you let me raise my knees a bit more and . . . Ooh, I see you *can,* and I must say it feels divine at that angle after so long without having a man in there at *any* angle."

He almost said he was glad he hadn't had any the night before too. But he didn't. She'd been right about the stories folks make up in bed together. It was less complicated to just let the loving tell its own sweet story. But damned if she didn't go on talking after he'd rolled her on her back to fuck her downright romantically.

Chapter 14

They were stuck up at Fort Hall the better part of a week because the dudes Longarm was supposed to ride herd on kept expecting Pocatello to settle for less than the fairer price he went on demanding no matter how many times they powwowed or how they asked old Wadzewipa to translate their cheaper offer. And Dame Flora wasn't about to turn back without Longarm's help in her search for those missing women.

Longarm didn't mind. Old Flora was even more fun in broad day, on pine needles, when they went riding now and again to exercise their ponies, they said. For the creamy-skinned Scotch gal was auburn-headed all over, and she said she enjoyed watching his shaft parting that pretty fuzz down yonder when he did it to her braced on arms as straight and stiff.

Aside from so much pleasure, the stay was good for his business as well. Thanks to the government telegraph and the leisure he had to use it free, Longarm was able to telegraph all over creation, and with some of the answers he had time to wait for, waiting for old Senator Rumford to raise the ante or fold, he was able to tidy up some of his own concerns without missing a meal or as many sessions of sweet slap and tickle as a lady might want.

Dame Flora seemed to want a lot of them. She said she was

sure old Angus was getting some of little Jeannie and didn't want her hired help to get ahead of her.

Murgatroid Westmore's memory improved wondrously as soon as Longarm was able to uncover his true name and all the other silly things he was remembered for back home in Tennessee. Longarm had little trouble convincing the surviving member of Tim McBride's gang that most any federal prison had to be an improvement on Tennessee State Prison, or that seeing he was sure to do more hard time on those old local wants than Uncle Sam was likely to give him, it was mighty dumb to hold out the pure shit on pals who were too dead to care whether one peached on them or not.

So once Westmore and some confirming wires had identified all the bodies in the springhouse for certain, the agency buried them a polite distance from their more respectable and hence respected dead Indians. Westmore was even willing to help with information on those other poor souls who'd crossed Longarm earlier, with such sad results. According to Westmore, W. R. Callisher, the crude cattle baron Longarm had shot it out with in the Burlington train shed, had been acting on his own as the stupid bastard everyone had said he was. All the other attempts on Longarm along the way had been inspired by Pappy, or Tim McBride, to keep a savvy lawman from doing just what Longarm had done in the end.

Westmore denied any knowledge of missing Scotch spinsters, moonshiners running corn to Indians, or Indians running smoke puffs up into the sky. Longarm decided his prisoner was likely telling the truth. He'd been holding out on Westmore just a mite. He'd meant what he said about forgetting to tell Tennessee he had their want on ice for them, provided Westmore wanted to cooperate. But he'd forgotten to tell Westmore about that murder warrant the state of Missouri had outstanding on a mean little bastard. He figured he might as well let that sheriff's deputy from Liberty, Missouri, tell Westmore once he got to Fort Hall. They likely owed the poor shit a few more days in Fool's Paradise for being so talkative.

Getting in touch with Zion County regarding the true names and records of those rascals in their potter's field was sort of complicated. Longarm decided to hold off until he passed through there on the way back. None of them would be going anywhere, and it hardly seemed likely anyone would ever want them dug up.

Since Dame Flora kept pestering him about those missing gals, when she wasn't pestering him to go riding with her, Longarm even got in touch with an old pal from Scotland Yard. It had been possible to cable London since just before the war, and while Scotland Yard was nowhere near Scotland, they did keep tabs on most all such shit anywhere in the British Isles.

His old pal, Inspector Fennel, who'd been looking for that mean Englishman in Colorado that time, wasn't able to tell Longarm and Dame Flora anything they hadn't already figured out, though.

As the pretty gal had already told Longarm, nobody could recall what the person or persons placing the classified proposals in the Scotch newspapers might have looked like. Fennel suggested by wire, and Longarm agreed, it hardly seemed likely nobody would recall a red Indian or even an obvious Yank. Dame Flora said she'd already had her Angus check that out. It seemed Angus had been a private detective she'd hired back home, first to see what he could find out for her there, and then to bodyguard her and Jeannie once she decided to track the missing spinsters all the way to the wilds of Deseret. She said his affair with her maid had started somewhere this side of the Mississippi and that she'd been feeling mighty left out, although her kind never dallied with the hired help, even when they were far better-looking than crusty old Angus.

Checking with the B.I.A. itself, Longarm had no trouble establishing Pete Robbins as a notorious pest who'd been run off more than a dozen times for running bad booze to wards of the government. A warrant signed by Judge Isaac Parker over to Fort Smith had likely inspired Robbins and his trash to run and keep running on learning Longarm was a deputy U.S. marshal. More than one such gent had been after them over in the Cherokee Strip a spell back.

And so, in sum, Longarm was more than anxious to get back into action by the time Senator Rumford and Chief Pocatello had agreed to disagree, for the rest of that year at least. Rumford got the Fort Hall agency to hide and hang on to all that silver for him so it wouldn't have to be packed all the way back again when, not if, the government agreed to Pocatello's terms. When plump Congressman Granger opined a couple of cold snaps would doubtless bring even a stubborn old savage to his senses, the older and far more talked-out Senator Rumford agreed with Longarm that Pocatello and that wise old medicine woman would be as likely to up the ante once they'd shown they could make it through another winter the same as ever.

So Dame Flora and her help tagged along, and even helped, when the dudes Longarm had to ride herd on headed back to civilization.

The going was faster now, because they didn't have to cope with overloaded mules. They still had to camp one night on the trail, to the delight of Dame Flora and likely Jeannie. Old Angus was a sort of husky cuss when you watched him splitting firewood in his shirtsleeves.

They all made it into Zion without anything more exciting than that taking place. By general agreement, everyone checked into the Overland overnight stop again. The stock was due for a good rest before pushing on down the delta in any case.

Longarm had meant to wait till after noon dinner to scout up the local authorities, figuring they'd be eating too. But Bishop Reynolds and that county coroner, Lukas, came over to pester him when they heard he was back in town. So Longarm joined them out in that big front room, saying, "I meant to come over to your courthouse later in the day."

Lukas said, "You'll be pleased to know we buried that poor gal you sent us over on the temple grounds. When those show folk told us you suspected she might be one of them missing Mormon brides, the bishop here said it seemed wrong to plant even a would-be Saint in Potter's Field."

Longarm nodded at the church elder and lawman and said, "That was neighborly of you, sir, and she really did come all this way to marry up with some Saint, or some son of a bitch who told her he was, before he helped himself to her dowry and murdered her the way he must have murdered others. The one we found was a Miss Una Munro. I got her home address and all written down somewhere. She didn't have anyone more likely to bury her decently than you Christian folks already have."

Lukas said, "Well, I never. I thought for certain she'd been killed by Indians. Them show folk told us you all found the body on Wagonwheel Hill, near the ashes of an Indian signal fire."

Longarm shrugged and said, "So someone wanted us to think. Only I think that that smoke talk was meaningless, and was designed to lead me to Miss Munro's body, just like it did. You don't have to be Indian to toss wet grass on a cow-chip fire, you know."

Lukas laughed uncertainly and said, "No argument about that. But why in thunder would anyone want you, a paid-up federal lawman, to find the body of a murdered woman on federal open range?"

"They hoped to keep me from suspecting where they'd planted her and all those others to begin with," Longarm answered laconically as he groped absently in his vest pockets while explaining. "Dame Flora MacSorley and her Scotch detective agency traced almost all those missing Scotch gals as far as the Mormon Delta, after which I suspect they were disappointed in love, considerably, by a suitor more interested in their dowry *dinero* than their fair white bodies."

As the two local men exchanged thunderstruck glances Longarm got out a cheroot, saying, "I'll ask you to forgive my manners this one time, Bishop. I get an awful green taste in my mouth every time I have to consider how sick at heart as well as terrified those poor slickered spinsters must have felt, at the end of such a long trail, when they discovered the man of their dreams was a nightmare out to murder and rob 'em."

"Those are monstrous charges as well!" Bishop Reynolds declared severely as Longarm fumbled for a waterproof match with his other hand.

Longarm seemed to be having trouble thumbnailing a light as he quietly observed, "I know. That's why I was meaning to mosey over to your courthouse this afternoon. Got to get me some snoop warrants. Got to find more evidence before I charge anybody with playing Bluebeard with all those Scotch bluebelles."

"Justice Atwell is a Saint who answers to me!" snapped Reynolds with a stern look at Longarm's unlit cheroot. He added in an even more imperious tone, "Just tell us where you'd like to search here in Zion County and I'll say yes or no."

Longarm finally got his match going as he replied with a thin smile, "*Bueno*. I'd start with your temple tithing ledgers, seeing you've offered to help."

The churchman and lawman got so excited Longarm shook his light out and said soothingly, "Now nobody but a total fool could expect a gang like this to keep written records of some insane plot. But wouldn't the temple tithe records give us the names of all the local Saints who ever sold land, stock, or supplies to anyone at any profit, along with the name of any buyer who might or might not have had a sensible explanation as to where he got the money?"

Bishop Reynolds scowled and said, "Of course." Then he showed he rated his badge as well by blinking thoughtfully and deciding, "By Moroni's golden tablets, I follow your logic!"

Coroner Lukas must have too. Seeing Longarm seemed to be lighting up, at last, with both hands, Lukas went for his gun.

Longarm had been hoping he might. So before the desperate Lukas could draw, the deadly little derringer he'd been palming for some time in his big right fist went off twice, point-blank, in the two-faced lover's contorted face!

Then Longarm let go of his spent derringer like a hot coal when he saw Bishop Reynolds slapping leather as well! Longarm's empty gun hand dove for an eternity through gun smoke thick as molasses in January as he sickly saw the older man was too quick on the draw to beat from half-so-far behind. But then the trusty Mormon's six-gun blazed more than once, and Longarm saw Reynolds wasn't aiming at *him* after all. So he crabbed farther from the line of fire as he got his own gun out, at last, to throw down on the stubby figure in the dining room archway he'd just had his back to.

He didn't fire. Nobody had to shoot old Angus again. For the Scotch detective simply dropped his .38 Bulldog with a twisted smile and buckled at the knees to follow it on down while Reynolds was marveling, "He was about to shoot you in the back, Deputy Long!"

Longarm bent to scoop up his empty derringer as he soberly said, "That's one I owe you and I sure feel stupid! For my pals in Scotland Yard *told* me someone who blended into a Scotch crowd must have placed all those proposals in Scotch newspapers!"

After that both doorways commenced to crowd up. Poor drab Jeannie, whom the two-faced Scotchman had been screwing, let out a hideous wail to see her Angus sprawled there in the clearing gunsmoke. She threw herself down on him like a sobbing and shuddering bed quilt.

When Dame Flora came out to join her, Longarm moved closer, warning, "Don't risk skunk blood on your own dress, ma'am. As we were just saying, a skunk working in cahoots with others to lure gals and their life savings all this way must have felt mighty slick when you advertised for help and he applied for the job."

Dame Flora protested, "But Angus really was a private investigator, with experience here in the West as a range detective and . . . *Och, mo Dai!* I see it all now!"

She didn't really. Nobody did before Longarm and Zion County rounded up all the Lukas help and impounded all the black-hearted bastard's business records. But after that it was simple. The inventive bookkeeping of a rapidly expanding beef baron who'd been buying way more than he'd been selling didn't meant frog spit as soon as one compared it with the more truthful church tithes of honest Mormon neighbors who'd offered exactly ten percent, no more, no less, of each and every sale to their county coroner.

Casually recorded deaths and burials failed to hold up also once one compared the Potter's Field burial of supposed male vagrants with the bones and above all *shoes* of Scotch females. Some of the frightened hands who'd helped to bury them were willing to fill in the fine print as soon as Bishop Reynolds said it seemed a shame they were just outside Utah Territory, where you got your choice between the gallows and a firing squad.

Billy Vail was as pleased with the final outcome, once Longarm got back to Denver. As they were jawing about it in Vail's office Vail chortled, "Senator Rumford wrote you a letter of commendation once he got back East. You done us proud by saving that silver for Uncle Sam and his Shoshoni wards."

Longarm reached for a smoke as an excuse to look away. What they didn't know about his own Indian policy wouldn't hurt any honest man and might help the Indians some.

Vail continued. "The governor of Missouri sent us a handsome thank you for the capture of Murgatroid Westmore, and the British Foreign Office thinks you saved Lord knows how many more subjects of their Queen from a fate worse than fucking. So there's only a single detail you failed to explain in your official report, old son."

When Longarm innocently asked what he'd left out, Vail demanded, "Where in blue blazes have you *been* all this time? Them dudes and even Murgatroid Westmore have been back East long enough for us to get wires about 'em."

Longarm lit his cheroot before he mildly suggested he'd had a few last loose ends to take care of out Utah way.

Vail grinned sort of dirty and decided, "I'll *bet* her end was loose by the time you were done with it. You never said in your report what that Dame Flora looked like, but . . ."

"Hold on. That high-toned Scotch lady and her maid left for the East aboard the same train as Rumford and those other dudes. So you ought to be ashamed of yourself, Billy Vail."

Vail said he'd meant no serious disrespect to a lady who knew Queen Victoria personally, but persisted. "Nobody left for nowhere before you and that Bishop Reynolds had tied up all the loose ends and solved the case entirely. So what, or *who* have you been dallying with since you parted company with those Scotch gals almost a full week ago, you rascal?"

Longarm didn't answer. That wistfully sweet young widow woman who'd managed that hotel in Ogden hadn't had a thing to do with any federal case, and he'd assured her the night Dame Flora and her maid had checked out that he'd never kiss and tell.

Watch for

LONGARM AND THE NIGHT BRANDERS

169th in the bold LONGARM series from Jove

Coming in January!

If you enjoyed this book, subscribe now and get...

TWO FREE

A $7.00 VALUE–

If you would like to read more of the very best, most exciting, adventurous, action-packed Westerns being published today, you'll want to subscribe to True Value's Western Home Subscription Service.

Each month the editors of True Value will select the 6 very best Westerns from America's leading publishers for special readers like you. You'll be able to preview these new titles as soon as they are published, *FREE* for ten days with no obligation!

TWO FREE BOOKS

When you subscribe, we'll send you your first month's shipment of the newest and best 6 Westerns for you to preview. With your first shipment, two of these books will be yours as our introductory gift to you absolutely *FREE* (a $7.00 value), regardless of what you decide to do. If

you like them, as much as we think you will, keep all six books but pay for just 4 at the low subscriber rate of just $2.75 each. If you decide to return them, keep 2 of the titles as our gift. No obligation.

Special Subscriber Savings

When you become a True Value subscriber you'll save money several ways. First, all regular monthly selections will be billed at the low subscriber price of just $2.75 each. That's at least a savings of $4.50 each month below the publishers price. Second, there is never any shipping, handling or other hidden charges—*Free home delivery*. What's more there is no minimum number of books you must buy, you may return any selection for full credit and you can cancel your subscription at any time. A TRUE VALUE!

A special offer for people who enjoy reading the best Westerns published today.

WESTERNS!

NO OBLIGATION

Mail the coupon below

To start your subscription and receive 2 FREE WESTERNS, fill out the coupon below and mail it today. We'll send your first shipment which includes 2 FREE BOOKS as soon as we receive it.